THE AUT[...]

Colin MacInnes was born in London in 1914. His mother, the formidable Angela Mackail, granddaughter of Burne-Jones, cousin of Kipling and Stanley Baldwin, later became famous as the novelist Angela Thirkell. His father was the singer James Campbell McInnes. Both Colin and his elder brother Graham, afterwards a writer and distinguished diplomat, had a stormy childhood: their parents' marriage foundered and in 1919 they set sail for Australia with Angela's new husband, George Thirkell. They settled in Melbourne and the boys did not see their natural father again for fifteen years. Both attended Scotch College, and at the age of sixteen Colin won a scholarship to Melbourne University, but went instead to work for the Imperial Continental Gas Association in Belgium. In 1936 he enrolled at the Chelsea Polytechnic to study art, continuing at the progressive Euston Road School; but with the outbreak of war he joined the Intelligence Corps, and saw active service in the wake of the Normandy Landings.

He wrote about his war experiences in *To the Victors the Spoils* (1950). This was followed two years later by *June in Her Spring*, the first of his Australian novels – *All Day Saturday* (1966) is the other; both are published by The Hogarth Press. His other books include the famous 'London' trio – *City of Spades* (1957), *Absolute Beginners* (1959) and *Mr Love and Justice* (1960) – and non-fiction such as *England, Half English* (1961). Throughout these years he was a controversial figure on the artistic and social scenes: as art critic for the *Observer*, one of the first participants in the BBC radio series 'The Critics', and as a commentator on black affairs, politics, music, literature, art and sexuality for, amongst others, *Encounter*, the *New Left Review*, and the *Spectator*; he was also a founding contributor to *New Society*. Colin MacInnes died in Hythe, Kent, in 1976 and was buried at sea off Folkestone.

ALL DAY
SATURDAY

Colin MacInnes

New Introduction by
Tony Gould

THE HOGARTH PRESS
LONDON

For
Nancy Shepherdson

Published in 1985 by
The Hogarth Press
40 William IV Street, London WC2N 4DF

First published in Great Britain by MacGibbon & Kee Ltd 1966
Copyright © The Colin MacInnes Estate 1966
Introduction copyright © Tony Gould 1985

The cover shows
Girl in pink. 1937
Ralph Balson 1890–1964
Gift of W. Balson
Art Gallery of New South Wales

British Library Cataloguing in Publication Data
MacInnes, Colin
All Day Saturday
I. Title
823'.914[F]   PR6063.A239
ISBN 0 7012 1012 5

Printed in Great Britain by
Cox & Wyman Ltd
Reading, Berkshire

INTRODUCTION

All Day Saturday was the second of the two novels Colin MacInnes wrote about Australia. The first, *June in Her Spring*, came out in 1952, before he had made a name for himself as the author of the three 'London' novels, *City of Spades*, *Absolute Beginners* and *Mr Love and Justice*. *All Day Saturday* did not appear until 1966, which prompts the question: what made MacInnes return to an Australian theme fourteen years after his earlier effort?

The most obvious reason for his renewed interest is that he had recently – in 1964 – been back to the country of his boyhood (he had lived there between the ages of six and sixteen) as the guest of Time Life Books, for whom he wrote the 'LIFE World Library' volume on Australia and New Zealand. Another incentive may have been the publication of his elder brother Graham McInnes's (spelt thus: Colin's was the deviant spelling of his surname) first book of memoirs of *his* Australian childhood, *The Road to Gundagai*, in 1965. A third likely explanation is a material one: namely, that by the mid-Sixties he was short of both money and inspiration and was looking to cash in on work which to some extent had already been done. His study of the music hall, *Sweet Saturday Night*, leans heavily on a series of BBC radio scripts he had written a decade earlier; and *All Day Saturday* derives from a radio play called 'The Baileys' which he had submitted to the BBC as long before as 1947 (they turned it down, damning it with faint praise of the 'of its kind, quite good' sort).

Since the play on which it is based pre-dates *June in Her Spring*, it is not surprising that *All Day Saturday* has much in common with *June*: the same setting among the squat-tocracy of Victoria's Western District in the 1920s, and many individuals who are more or less interchangeable. Walter

Bailey in this novel and Nathan Westley in *June* are both withdrawn and suicidal; the girl Maureen is certainly first cousin to the eponymous heroine of *June*; Julius Macnamara resembles Henry Bond in his depravity, if not in his skill on the 'goanna'; and Norman Culley, like Arthur Westley, is a 'larrikin'. Unlike Arthur, however, Norman is successful: not a social misfit, but the perfection of a type, 'lithe, tough, mindless and delinquent'. And to understand Australian ambivalence about delinquency one need look no further than to the mythological status accorded to Ned Kelly.

All Day Saturday owes its origin to an incident recounted by Graham McInnes in his second volume of memoirs, *Humping My Bluey*, which, by an ironic coincidence, appeared only months before *All Day Saturday*. Graham writes of the time when he was sixteen and Colin just fourteen and both, as usual, had been shunted off to the country for the summer holidays by their mother, Angela Thirkell. He is describing the round-the-world 'All Red Route' which aimed to link the mother country by wireless to the great dominions of Canada and Australia; to this end there had been built 'the spidery three-hundred-foot tall lattice towers of the "beam wireless"' at Ballan:

Colin and I had once been invited to spend a weekend at 'the beam' with the engineers and as a special treat mounted to the top of one of the enormously tall towers. I horrified them all, including myself in retrospect, by crawling out along the lateral beam which capped the tower like the cross-bar of a T and there singing 'It Had To Be You' suspended three hundred feet over the iron-hard grass . . .

The most striking thing about *All Day Saturday* is how it resembles an Angela Thirkell novel turned upside down: not only geographically, with the Victorian squattocracy replacing the English aristocracy – or county folk (each, though, having the characteristics of a closed society or charmed world) – but also in the treatment of the subject matter. Like a Thirkell novel, it is about love, and young love in particular. But whereas the older women in Angela Thirkell's novels are poised and know just how to deflect the 'calf love' they inspire, in *All Day Saturday* it is an older woman who makes a fool of herself in pursuit of the young larrikin. In Thirkell novels the older people are wise and tolerant of the foibles of youth; in *All Day Saturday* the situation is reversed: the false wisdom of the older people is tellingly contrasted with the instinctive good sense of the young – of Maureen, in particular:

. . . surprising herself at rebuking a man she had hitherto held somewhat in awe, and realising yet again (as she had come to do more and more) that those older than herself were not always so 'wise' as they had so often implied to her they were . . .

Oh, the older generation, Maureen thought once again! Will I ever be as dopey as they are when I get to be their age? No self-control – well, that doesn't matter so much (who has it, anyway?) – but not even any sense of what they want and what they don't. Honestly, I'm beginning to think 'experience' simply means you get softer and sillier every time the same thing happens to you all over again!

Yet this novel is also a kind of back-handed tribute to mother (who had died three or four years before MacInnes wrote it, though mother and son had been estranged for many years before that): there are echoes of Thirkell in the whole treatment of the mating-game as well as in particular snatches of witty dialogue, such as this exchange between the brazen young Nancy and the fat, middle-aged Mrs Baxter:

'Nancy, I think you're a slut.'
'And what are you?'
'An older woman is never a slut – she's just a misfortune.'

The review of *All Day Saturday* which pleased MacInnes most was by D.A.N. Jones in the *New Statesman*. Jones likened the novel to a Jacobean tragi-comedy and demonstrated how chunks of both narrative and dialogue could be set out as blank verse – 'lusty, beautiful people,' he wrote, 'indulge their wilful passions, speak in a high, artificial style, pose like figures in an allegory.'

All Day Saturday is less sensuous and idyllic than *June in Her Spring*, but it is also less flawed. There is no equivalent to the insistence on heredity which mars *June*; and there is, in addition to the taut drama (MacInnes was very proud of himself for having preserved the classical 'unities', for having contained the action within a single day) which culminates on a tiny square metal platform at the summit of a radio mast hundreds of feet above the ground, a sustained attempt to get at the essential 'Australianness' of Australians:

As is the Australian custom, the men soon drifted together and if they addressed the women, were matey to them as if they were males of a different sub-species; for though their country is uninhibited about sex, it has no conception of sexual mystery, glamour or romance.

And yet, these people *were* in a sense glamorous. They had a vigour, a physical perfection, a confidence, a youthful hope despite their cynicism, that have vanished from the ancient world. At rare moments in history, by a series of accidents never to be repeated, there flower societies in which the cult of *happiness* is paramount: hedonistic, mindless, intent upon the glorious physical instant! And such a benison has fallen, for a decade or so (and despite the recently remembered horrors of Gallipoli and Ypres), on this generation protected by the seemingly fixed radiance of the kind sun and the nocturnal brilliance of the Southern Cross.

Both McInnes brothers have left descriptions of the social scene on the fringe of the Western District, where they spent such memorable summer holidays. This is the view Graham expresses in *The Road to Gundagai*:

. . . one quickly discovered, even in democratic rural Australia, that two classes existed. On the one hand, were the station owners and their town guests, the professional men from Ballan, the doctor, the lawyer, the engineers of the local wireless transmitting station and one or two marginal farmers who went in for mixed sheep and wheat or fruit, and were therefore considered on the verge of being respectable. On the other hand were the roustabouts and boundary riders from the sheep stations, the railway folk, the workers in the little town and the local phenomenon known as the 'cocky' farmer. This really meant, in European terms, a peasant yeoman, although no Australian would ever admit it. He was usually a dour independent cranky kind of fellow whom one saw with one foot up on a wire fence peering morosely into the middle distance with a short pipe stuck between his teeth.

Here by contrast, is Colin's view, expressed early on in this novel:

J. G. Eaton and Tommy Mulligan were the only two engineers at the radio station whom the district had accepted. Being 'accepted' by the district – that is, getting onto the circuit of the local squattocracy – is not a matter of having money, let alone brains (though these don't disqualify), nor of being what is known as a gentleman. (There are no gentlemen, anyway, in the English sense, in the whole vast continent of Australia – a great relief to one and all.) What you must have, to be accepted, is a certain kind of *style*. For example, of the Hackett family down by the Glen, Leo was okay but his brothers and parents not – and most certainly not his sisters or his brothers' wives [for a fuller account of the Hacketts, see *June in Her Spring*]. This is snobbery of a kind, but based on something valid if impossible to define – '*Is he all right?*' Your accent and income and job can all be wrong, and yet you can be 'all right' to the district in this sense. (They can all also be right, and you can be all wrong.)

The point is not which, if either, of these versions is correct, but the difference they reflect in the approaches of the two brothers. Graham's – oddly enough, in view of Colin's reputation in this field – is the more sociological; Colin's – not so surprisingly, given the genre he is working in – the more novelistic. But there is more to it than that. Colin's antipathy to the whole notion of class was largely, no doubt, a reaction to his mother's obsession with it; but it was a key factor in both his life and his art, and accounts for the cult appeal of his most popular novel, *Absolute Beginners*. If the message of that novel could be reduced to a slogan, it would be: Down with class, up with style.

A large part of the attraction of Australia, at least in retrospect, for Colin MacInnes was its freedom from class restraints, its egalitarianism. And *All Day Saturday*, like *June in Her Spring* before it, is a celebration of that freedom.

Tony Gould, London 1984

ALL DAY SATURDAY

MRS HELEN BAILEY was the *femme fatale* of the district, but nobody minded about this much. The men didn't mind because there could be no doubt Helen was a *wonderful woman*, her beauty excusing her advancing years, and a perfect hostess at her husband Walter Bailey's station, Cootamundra—and then she (or he) was rich. Also, it must be said, the men of the district, whether sheep farmers or engineers at the nearby international radio installation, were randy in their hard way but did not much relish love affairs: they loved their work, their wives, and the odd sheila down at Melbourne for the races, in that order. So they were pleased and content that Helen should be the non-operative queen bee of the area, though it's true some of them hinted she was a cock-teaser.

As for the women, they were even more benevolent. They had long recognized Helen was not a rival in any effective sense, and they gazed at her sterile, rather desperate flirtations with wide, understanding, tolerant (or indifferent) eyes. Also, it was fitting that the neighbourhood should have a great lady who was its focal point without being a cause of serious dispute. What is more, a lot of them liked Helen: it was hard not to. For she was kind and patient and solicitous—hers was always the first phone call in times of trouble, the thoughtful letter (nobody else in the district ever wrote letters of more than one half page), the helpful descent from her Armstrong-Siddeley bearing passion-fruit and a ready ear. The women of the district, in fact, were proud of Helen: not every area in the sheep country had as unmistakable a personality for its centre of social gravity as she.

Yet the paradox was that though the district flocked to the Saturday tennis and picnics and balls at Cootamundra, it was a lonely place: you had only to look at it to see this instantly. There it stood, up on the metallic plateau, with the eight high steel masts of the radio station set diagonally in groups of four on the horizon (beaming out their messages to the world), and with its rambling house that was opulent if not luxurious, and its paraphernalia of adjacent sheep buildings (from which emanated a constantly faint whiff of greasy wool), and its cracked tennis courts (all four of them), and its garages with their own petrol bowsers, and its home orchard and vegetable gardens (not so many flowers)—and it was desolate. Perhaps it was the plateau: for there are some places on the earth in which human creatures are not designed to dwell. Or perhaps it was the lack of water, which had caused the Bailey family, when they first squatted there, to build those corrugated iron tanks high up on struts and wooden platforms, and later metal windmills, to suck what moisture they could from the forbidding soil. Or perhaps it was the personal drama of Helen and Walter Bailey that no one ever referred to amid the shouts and jumps and guzzlings and boozings of every Saturday throughout the sunny season of the year.

For Walter Bailey *never appeared*. You could visit his house a hundred times and never see him, except by accident. Very occasionally he did take part in tennis (he had been, in his youth, a champion) and startled everybody as much by his very presence as by his skill and silence. But mostly, when he was not out supervising the station (more usually on horseback than in a car), he shut himself up in the annexe to the main building, and did there nobody quite knew what. People, indeed, had given up asking Helen 'And how is Walter?' when they visited Cootamundra, or inviting him as well if Helen Bailey was bidden to a nearby station. It was long taken for granted that Walter Bailey —though so hospitable indirectly, for who in the district had not enjoyed the products of his station?—that Walter wished to keep himself to himself, and this wish was respected.

Gossip about the reasons for this situation had long died down: if a new face appeared in the area it might revive again, but the topic was so well-worn that discussion of it soon fell into well-accepted grooves. There was the theory that Helen and Walter lived apart because they had never had a baby; but this notion carried scant conviction, for was there not in the district many a childless couple who hit it off despite this personal disaster? There was the theory Helen had married Walter not for love, but money, and that this had turned him sour against her. That she had done so was undeniable, for Helen came from the city (which, to the district, always betokens poverty—the district simply will not believe that wealth can exist without a sheep an acre), yet several fruitful marriages in the area had been based on such a union of wealth and beauty. The hopeful notion that Walter had a secret mistress was dismissed, since you cannot have a secret mistress in the district, and he hardly ever left it year in and year out. The corollary theory, enticing at first, that Helen had a surreptitious lover somewhere was also soon rejected, for Helen was far too transparent, virginal, for this to be.

Then why did they stay together? the new arrival in the district would enquire. To this the collective wisdom of the district would return the answer that up here, people do stay together: they don't run away, or take world trips, or set up separate houses because the rhythm of the life here would make this ridiculous: you can't fit in unless you stick it out. There are passions in the district, but no dramas: there is no place whatever for the odd man, or woman, out.

★

The solitude at Cootamundra was muted by the presence of the girls: Maureen and Nancy, of equal age, the one blonde (Nance) and the other vaguely brown. The function of these girls, who were quite unrelated to the Baileys, was to be Helen's 'companions'; and without them, she felt she would certainly have gone mad.

Maureen accepted this servitude, and Nance did not. According to Maureen, it was far better to live out at Cootamundra, in relative affluence with a lot of parties, than to pig it down at the fruit farm with her brothers. Besides, Maureen liked Helen Bailey—and even liked old Walter, in a way, at the rare times she saw him. She liked Helen because the older woman was sweet to her as no one else had ever been, and this was a quality Maureen prized, believing it to be rare. As for Nance, she did not care for Helen at all. Her notion was that Helen used her and Maureen not as 'companions' at all, but as decoy ducks for enticing local men. But as Nancy had every grim intention of marrying one of these, she accepted the situation too.

There arise, in the district, mornings so splendid that even though you know the later afternoon will be a terrible bake, the promise of those radiant early hours redeems the day. And Nancy and Maureen, that Saturday, had carried out their orange juice and corn flakes onto the large shady back veranda. They were both in pyjamas, and both smoking that glorious first fag of the day that lifts your head, instead of eating. Being in the cool of the veranda was like sitting in a cinema gazing at another unreal world. For away outside, the glaze shimmered off the parched paddocks stretching far off towards the radio masts, and the sheep were already taking shelter from the sun beneath the shrivelled eucalyptuses.

'J G phoned,' said Nancy.

'What was he on about?'

'He says, can be bring a boy over for the tennis this afternoon.'

'I bet you said yes.'

'Too true I did. Though mind you, he's not a local boy. He's J G's nephew or cousin or something up from the capital.'

'So Tommy will drive them both over.'

'If he's not too drunk to.'

J G Eaton and Tommy Mulligan were the only two engineers at the radio station whom the district had accepted. Being 'accepted' by the district—that is, getting onto the circuit of the local squattocracy—is not a matter of having money, let alone brains (though these don't disqualify), nor of being what is known as a gentleman. (There are no gentlemen, anyway, in the English sense, in the whole vast continent of Australia—a great relief to one and all). What you must have, to be accepted, is a certain kind of *style*. For example, of the Hackett family down by the Glen, Leo was okay but his brothers and parents not— and most certainly not his sisters or his brothers' wives. This is a snobbery of a kind, but based on something valid if impossible to define—'*Is he all right?*' Your accent and income and job can all be wrong, and yet you can be 'all right' to the district in this sense. (They can all also be right, and you can be all wrong).

J G Eaton, undoubtedly a brainy engineer, made it at once with the district since, by the way he treated them, he took it so completely for granted that they *would* accept him. A good-natured man, and very popular (though playing a frightful game of tennis), he had two grave, if minor, defects. He had once served on a radio station on a Pacific island, with two other men only who were not relieved until after a year, by which time one of them had gone berserk. That was all right, but J G Eaton, particularly when in his cups, would tell the tale over and over again. The other cause of ennui was when J G told you about his woman Margaret, at present up in Queensland, who was shortly coming down south to marry him. Margaret, according to J G, was a paragon in whom nobody could quite believe, and her arrival in the district was awaited with some dismay.

11

J G's pal Tommy Mulligan was a real boozer—one of those men who make liquor a substitute for sex. But he remained sober when on duty (though with truly ghastly hangovers) and was so kind and equable (albeit a trifle melancholy) that the district took him to its heart—especially the men. 'Good old Tommy,' they would say, with that particular sort of tenderness tough extroverts reserve for a vulnerable erring sheep.

'And this boy's J G's nephew, you say.'

'Or cousin, or something.'

'Has he got a name?'

'It was Norman Culley, J G said.'

'Culley?'

'That's what it sounded like over the tinkler.'

Maureen ruminated. She was not, like Nancy, determined to get her man whoever he might be. But Maureen had a dream, a vision, of a marvellous young feller who would one day come and claim her. This did not mean Maureen was what is known as a 'romantic' (though even if she was, romanticism has its own pointers to reality)—in fact she was more hard-headed far than Nance who, truth to tell, was a sharp-witted scatterbrain with such a bright eye for the main chance she would be almost sure to miss it. It was rather that Maureen was, as some girls are (not many), *entire*: capable of total devotion, and consequently of total folly. So she had not hitherto been allured by any of the young males in the district—not because she didn't like them (she was very popular though a bit remote), but because none was the feller of her imaginings. (By the way, as to what this boy might be *like*, she was extremely imprecise; but she was quite sure she would recognize him when he came).

'Culley,' she said to Nance. 'It's a funny sort of a name.'

'Yep. By the bye, do you know something? I saw *him* this morning.'

(This was how Walter was referred to by the girls.)

'You didda? What was he up to?'

Nancy, to whom a long sentence was an effort, collected her scattered thoughts.

'He was crouching,' she said slowly, 'down by the big water tank behind his denizen' (this was what Nancy called Walter's annexe), 'tapping away at the rungs, to see how much water's left inside, I suppose.'

'But there's a gauge outside to demonstrate.'

'Nevertheless, girl, he was tapping: and what's more, muttering to himself.'

'Well, he's nervous about the water: that's why he's cut us all down to two inches only in the baths.'

'He's no reason to be nervous: the reserves in the big dams are ample, and the drought's due to break any day now.'

'He's just cautious; and I suppose it *is* his station, anyway.'

'Oh, granted.'

'And what's more, droughts never break when they're supposed to; and I can't see you, Nance, drinking yellow dam water, even boiled.'

Nancy pressed out her cigarette upon a bottle ant on the wood floor. 'Oh, granted once again,' she said. 'But if you ask me, babe, water or no water, he's going rapidly round the bend.' She rose, looking really rather stunning, stretched her arms and and yawned. 'Oh cripes, I wish I could get away from this hell of a futile place.'

★

When Helen Bailey rose, in the morning, from her lonely and beautiful triple bed, she looked, even at her age and at this hour, like Aphrodite stepping from the sea. That is to say, there was something *legendary* about Helen's looks and, more particularly her body: it was timeless and, despite her faults, ideal. Also, when she awoke, forgetting a while the miseries of her existence, she never failed to experience an initial moment of pure wonder: of joy at being herself, and a perpetual unquenchable hope that splendour and a kind donation of her heart and self would that day be her fortune. This first euphoria was of course swiftly followed by a thousand recollections of causes for complete dismay. Yet none such could dim the golden light that descended on Helen in her waking hour.

She gazed, as was her wont, at the photograph of Walter, and wondered for the billionth time what had gone wrong. For she had loved Walter, and still did, despite their catastrophe; and she believed Walter, despite everything, still loved her. Then why this total, perpetual wall between them—a barrier harder than any hatred could be, since they never quarrelled and neither had ever said a word of separation? What was the deep continuing bond, if they really meant absolutely nothing to each other?

Helen also examined a photograph of herself, taken at the time of her young marriage. With truth she could say she had hardly changed—yet perhaps therein lay, precisely, a clue to the whole trouble. For after so long a life with Walter she surely should have changed, if he had shared it.

She patted her hair to the style of this photograph of twenty years ago and adjusted the bosom of her nightdress to the low-cut yet decorous angle that had been modish in those days. Then she strolled about the room as if a fashion model, or a débutante at her first ball, pausing to strike poses, and catching sight of herself (as if by accident) in the tall mirrors that decorated the room. She felt an elation that conquered all her loneliness and despair until, out of the side window, she noticed the two girls going down with brooms to sweep the wind-driven leaves from off the tennis courts. And though she was not jealous of the girls—she truly wished them well, if only her own life could have beauty and fulfilment too—she felt a great pang at their youth and far more hopeful possibility of bliss. 'Oh, Helen,

Helen,' she said softly to herself, and great tears started suddenly from her huge eyes.

*

Walter Bailey, in his gun-room, was writing up his diary. If Walter were to die, and this diary be read by curious eyes, it would tell them nothing whatever about him save that he was methodical. For this record, though detailed, was of the barest facts and never did he express in it a comment or emotion.

His entry completed, Walter rose and walked round his little kingdom: for the annexe, though consisting only of two rooms and 'offices', and though sparsely, even austerely, furnished, contained all Walter needed for his comfort. Walter was not a puritan, and liked the opulent stations of his fellow sheep owners he sometimes visited. It was just that, by taste, he was naturally monkish and, for himself, believed simplicity to be the height of luxury. There may also have been an atavistic instinct to recover, round about him, the frugalities of his ancestor who, two generations back, had first staked out the Bailey claim to Cootamundra.

He thought of Helen—with remorse, yet with severity. (Their obsessive daily morning thoughts about each other were now their nearest to communion.) Their failure had been his fault —yes, that he admitted—but Helen was the cause of his being in error. No woman should have failed to return, *in the way he wished*, a love so great as his had been! He could forgive Helen the disaster of their marriage, but not that she had failed to see the depth of his nobility. Foolish, wanton, spendthrift woman, destroyer of an immense joy denied! Yet though Walter knew full well that they would now never be united, he believed so passionately in the possibility which had once existed, that this was still almost a reality. His strong lean frame crossed once more to the writing-desk and the diary which he re-opened, and there inscribed:

The solution lies in massive irrigation; but this is too expensive.

There was an abrupt loud spluttering and, gazing out from the window with annoyance, Walter saw J G Eaton getting out of a car and opening its bonnet. Walter was irritated both because J G was using not the main drive, but the side road leading past his annexe, and also because, being despite his taciturnity a man true by hereditary impulse to the basic rule of hospitality in the district, he knew he would have to go out and offer to lend J G a helping hand. Walter didn't mind the guests who flocked to his house, provided he didn't have to see them; but if some emergency occurred (as for instance when, years ago, Julius Macnamara had broken his fat foolish leg in the swimming pool), ancestral voices summoned Walter from his solitude to lend his reluctant aid.

So he walked slowly out of the annexe to confront J G Eaton's bottom as he plunged among the innards of his vehicle. 'Something wrong?' Walter Bailey asked the engineer.

As a matter of fact, J G Eaton was one of the few Walter Bailey could get on with. He had the initial advantage of being a stranger to the district, a bird of passage not privy to its stories and its secrets, and was therefore more innocuous. Also J G was so breezy and so amiably tactless, that he almost refused to recognize that Walter Bailey's attitude was in any way peculiar; and not to recognize a human problem is often, in some senses, to reduce it.

'Oh, hul-lo!' cried J G spinning abruptly round and beaming on Walter Bailey. 'What do you think, Mr Bailey? This is a new car, specially bought for Margaret, and lo and behold the first trip I make with the damn thing, it conks out on me.'

Walter gave a slight smile, said nothing and gazed into the

engine. 'Your carburettor's flooded,' he said. 'It may be leaking.'

'But on a new car. It can't be.'

'Let's have a look inside. Yes, it is. If you take it down to the men's quarters one of them will solder it for you.'

'And to think,' said J G, 'that I'm an engineer! Still, radio is my speciality, not cars. To tell you the truth, Mr Bailey, this is the first one I've ever actually owned. It's my eyes, you see.' J G peered at his reluctant host through owlish spectacles. 'Hitherto they've always failed me, but what with Margaret coming I felt we *must* have a vehicle, and took the test again and just got by.'

'Margaret is your intended?'

'Indeed she is, Mr Bailey. I haven't seen you before to tell you all about her, but hasn't Helen mentioned her at all?'

At the sound of his wife's name Walter twitched slightly, and even J G realised he had crossed a forbidden threshold. 'I hope you'll be happy with her,' Walter said, coldly and without conviction.

'Oh, but I will. How can I fail to be with a girl like Margaret? We're just made for each other and, believe it or not, Mr Bailey, she adores me—me!'

J G stood looking genuinely surprised. Walter nodded curtly, though not with unkind intent. 'Take it down to the workshop by the shearing sheds,' he said. 'The men will fix it for you.' With which he bowed slightly to J G and strode, round-shouldered, into the darkness of the annexe.

'A queer old coot,' said J G to himself, shaking his head sadly, for he loved the human race, and liked it to be happy. 'A queer old coot if ever there was one.'

He yanked out the carburettor, and started down the track. Passing the tennis courts, there was a great yell from Nance of 'J G, what the hell have you come over for so early?'

He detoured towards the girls who, exhausted already by

their labours, were smoking in the summer-house beside the courts.

'Hullo–ullo!' he cried. 'Gosh, but you're both looking pretty. But not so winsome, please believe me, as my Margaret is. Just wait till you see her, the pair of you, and you'll be green with envy.'

Maureen smiled and Nancy sighed. 'We'll take your word for it, J G,' she said. 'But what brings you over here so soon?'

'Simply,' J G replied, 'that on the spur of the moment I thought you girls might need a helping hand with getting the buffet lunch ready, and I'm an expert, as you know, in cutting bread and slicing ham and peeling boiled potatoes.'

'You're not, you know, J G,' said Nancy. 'You're blind as a bat and guaranteed to mess everything up . . . and anyway, how the hell did you get over here? Are you alone?'

J G presented the carburettor. 'I came over with this,' he said, 'and what goes with it. I've got a car, now, Nance. And what's more'—J G gleamed in triumph—'I've got a licence!'

'Gawd! The government must be crazy! There'll be Death on the Road, my lad, with you around. But what about this boy you mentioned to me earlier? Has he come with you?'

'No, no, no. He'll be driving over with Tommy Mulligan later in the day.'

'But he's your relative, not Tommy's—why didn't *you* bring him over?'

At this point J G Eaton assumed a somewhat grave expression. 'He was incapable,' he answered, 'of so doing.'

'Doing what? He's sick, then, this boy?'

'Norman,' said J G earnestly, 'went down to the township last evening with Tommy M, and both were brought back to the radio station, incapacitated, by good friends.'

'That's not unusual for Tommy.'

'But the boy, Nance, is only twenty-two. So that apart from

his getting dead drunk being ridiculous, he's too young for that sort of thing.'

'He sounds a lively character, this relative of yours.'

J G Eaton frowned. 'As a matter of fact,' he said, 'I think I should warn you he's a bit of a delinquent.'

'Oh—ho! The black sheep of the family, J G. The guilty secret of the Eaton clan.'

'He's not a very *close* relative of mine.'

'Now, now, J G—don't you deny him thrice. You've asked him up here, haven't you? So you've got to take responsibility for him.'

'He asked himself up, as a matter of fact. He said he wanted to see what the sheep district was like, and I could scarcely refuse, though what with Margaret coming, it's inconvenient . . .'

Maureen had been silent, but now asked J G, 'But what's he like, this boy?'

'Like, Maureen? Well, let's take his good points first. He's an athlete, he's bold as brass—I'd say brash's a better word—and he's intelligent, no doubt about it. On the other hand he's ugly, sly, a liar and not to be relied upon in any way.'

'I must say,' said Nancy, 'you give him a good reference. Can he dance?'

'When he's not drinking, yes, he dances very well.'

'Does he like girls?' said Maureen.

'I expect so, but he principally likes himself.'

At this point Helen Bailey made one of her entrances. Now in these 'entrances' of Helen's (which annoyed Nancy exceedingly), there was no calculation, or hardly any: it just was that Helen seemed incapable of appearing among her fellow creatures without their becoming, for an instant, actors in a play of which she was the star. Perhaps the secret lay in Helen's sense of the dramatic: for all her life which was, in fact, God knows, drab enough, seemed to her if not a performance, at any rate a dress rehearsal.

'Oh J G, how nice, how sweet of you to come so early!' Helen cried, bestowing on the engineer a dazzling glance. To this J G responded with the instinct Helen aroused in most male breasts, which was that of *chivalry*; they longed to be her knight-errant, if not actually to possess her.

'Mrs Bailey,' said the engineer, 'you're looking ravishing—that's the word, I think. At all events it's the only one that fits.'

'And Margaret,' said Helen Bailey, seating herself in the summer-house as if on a cloud. 'What news of her?'

'I can't wait,' said J G earnestly, 'to bring you two together, Mrs B. For two reasons, that is, apart from general sociability. First that—with all respect to the girls here—her looks are worthy of your own . . . though yours, of course, are of a maturer mould—and none the worse for that,' J G added with unusually gallant haste. 'The next is, Mrs Bailey, I do want you please to sponsor her, and help launch her in the district. The district, you see,' he went on reflectively, 'will easily accept an unattached male, such as myself. But with women, I've noticed they're rather more chary—and they even might be with a lovely girl like Margaret. But with you to back her, Mrs Bailey, she can't go wrong. She'll be right in the plum centre of the magic circle.'

Helen, who wasn't altogether pleased with parts of this oration, laid her hand on J G's arm. 'Any friend of yours, J G,' she said, 'is also one of mine. And anyone so dear and close to your heart is doubly so, believe me.'

Nancy threw a tennis ball at a lizard, missing it narrowly. Maureen arose and wandered off to sweep more leaves at the far end of the dusty court.

*

Across the flinty paddocks of the plateau, Tommy Mulligan's car travelled along the rutted track that linked the radio station with the outer world. At the next gate Tommy slowed down, and waited for Norman Culley to get out and open it.

'What about your hopping out for a change?' said Norman Culley.

'Passenger's job, son. Driver sticks to his wheel.'

'Well, I can drive.'

'Let's see your licence.'

'Licence? You need a licence up here in these wilds?'

'It's the law, son. So out you hop.'

'It's too bloody hot. What so they have all these gates for, anyway?'

'To separate the flocks, son. Sheep must not mate with the wrong sheep, or the wool clip would doubtless suffer.'

'Well, why not automatic gates, then? Can't someone invent one?'

'They do exist . . . you run your wheel over a whatsit and a chain pulls the gate open. Closed by the same process on the further side. But the only station I know that's got them around here is old Julius Macnamara's.'

'Whose land is this, then?'

'Bailey's already. It's the biggest station in the area, if not the richest.'

'Which *is* the richest?'

'Macnamara's, though it's smaller. He's got the artesian wells and lusher pastures. Also, they say, he's invested his winnings in the capital, and not put it all back into barren land like most of them do up here . . . Now what about that gate?'

'And what about a drink? It's the only cure I know for a hangover.'

'Beer's on the back seat. Help yourself and me.'

Norman cracked two bottles with his teeth as the sun beat down on the canvas hood and the heat crackled, in a black glare, off the yellowed pastures.

'And who is this bird Macnamara?' Norman asked.

'A bit of a mystery man. Chiefly because he lives with this woman, Mrs Baxter.'

'And who's she when she's at home?'

'His housekeeper.'

'Well, what's so wrong with that?'

'Only that it's unusual. Rich men don't have housekeepers up here, they have wives.'

'She his tart, then?'

'That's what's supposed. On the other hand, it's also doubted.'

'How come? When a man and woman live together, don't they make it, usually?'

'She's about his age, which is middle-aged, and she's fat and lost her looks. If Julius wanted a sheila, he could do himself rather better than that.'

'Will they be over there today?'

'He will—he goes everywhere. She doesn't come out much—he keeps her in purdah at his station.'

'In whatta?'

'Never mind—just finish that beer and open up that gate.'

Norman took a lengthy swig. 'Will there be lots of them over there this afternoon?' he asked.

'It's thirty or forty usually on a Saturday . . . about that—sometimes fifty, you never can tell. Helen doesn't invite them specially—they all just know it's open house.'

'And how long does all this go on for?'

'There's tennis, then swimming in the big dam, then usually dancing till the smaller hours . . . it's well into Sunday before most of them get home to milk the cows and go to chapel . . .'

Norman, a little overawed (but not much) at the thought of this rural aristocracy, was silent, then said carefully, 'And these girls you spoke of—Nancy and Maureen. They nice?'

The engineer turned slowly round. 'You keep your hands off Nancy, son,' he said.

'What makes you say that? You sweet on her?'

'I'm going to marry her.'

'Does she know that?'

'Not yet she doesn't . . . but she will. As for Maureen, she wouldn't look at you.'

'Pleased with herself, is she?'

'She's just got taste: and judgement, son.'

Norman smiled sourly, and heaved himself out of the car. He threw his bottle at a rock (a sheep would wound its cleft hoof later on the jagged splinters), then leant on the car door. 'And Mrs Helen Bailey?' he enquired.

'She? As I've already told you, son, Mrs Bailey's a special case.'

There was something in Tommy's tone that made the lad think perhaps she really was. He smiled again showing his gapped teeth, his lips twisting and his eyes slanting, then shambled off towards the metal barrier. He moved in a taut, hunched way that was nevertheless relaxed, kicking stones as he went, and opening the gate with a minimum effort and much use of his feet—which were large and, despite his slender body, solid on the ground.

*

It was not often Mrs Baxter sulked: she didn't dare to. For materially, she depended totally on Julius Macnamara and his whims. On a visit to the capital, ages ago, Julius had found her managing the temperance hotel at which, by a quirk of avarice (for he was quite a heavy boozer), he liked to stay: liked to, perhaps, because he could lord it at this place in a way that would have been impossible in the grander hosteleries of the city. For though Julius was rich by the standards of the district, he could not compete with the magnates of the capital, nor with the really big landowners from up in New South Wales.

One night, before departing back to his estates, Julius, without

23

prior warning (and without having shown, previously, any special interest in her), had invited Mrs Baxter to the theatre to see the popular musical comedy of that year called *Chu Chin Chow*. She had enjoyed this outing, and the Chinese meal that (appropriately) had followed it, down in the alley known as 'Chink Street', or 'Little Lon'; and having been herself, in her young days, connected with the theatre (in which the late Mr Baxter worked front of house), and at that time what was in a woman deemed to be rather 'fast', she expected Julius, on their return to the temperance hotel, to try to seduce her: for which she was quite willing, provided the present—or at any rate his conduct—were all right. But when he took her to his private sitting-room, he had made no efforts in this direction but instead had suggested she might care to leave the hotel and come and housekeep for him at his station up in the sheep district. 'I can promise you an assured position, my dear,' he had said, 'and the opportunity to save a bit for your old age.'

With visions of wills and gifts, and of that domination which an astute woman, even with every initial disadvantage, can usually come to exercise over a man, however recalcitrant, if they live in daily close proximity, Mrs Baxter had accepted. But she had reckoned without the immense fund of endlessly patient obstinacy that she had not as yet divined in Julius Macnamara's temperament. For Julius, throughout the subsequent years, had kept her firmly in her place: she had nice rooms, plenty to eat and drink, adequate menial help, a little runabout car of her own (or rather, on loan to her, and she always felt he'd given it so as not to be obliged himself to give her lifts), and reasonable if not lavish wages—yet *housekeeper* was what she had been forced to remain at Macnamara's station. There were rooms, for instance, that she could not enter without knocking; and early attempts to discover any of Julius's plans—let alone participate in their determination—had been instantly frustrated. Julius made it crystal clear to her that however useful she was to him, if it came to a showdown he could easily do without her. But she, at her age, could no longer do without him, or his conditional largesse.

So after initial tantrums, she accepted her lot: aided by being a woman of profound good sense, if limited intelligence and imagination. If Julius was king at Macnamara's, and she most certainly was not queen, she was at any rate a substantial personage on the station. Those who had favours to seek from Julius soon discovered she could be a helpful intermediary—or the contrary, if crossed. And as for the district, if it did not exactly accept her in her own right, it did insofar as she was its richest citizen's acknowledged major-domo.

The cause of her sulks this Saturday arose from a highly peculiar conversation Julius had had with her the evening before. He had summoned her late at night to his 'study' (where all he 'studied' were station accounts and bound copies of *La Vie Parisienne* imported direct from Europe over the years), and had surprisingly offered her a port from one of two bottles, the first of which was already empty. Then, without preliminaries, he had dropped his bombshell. 'My dear,' he had said caressingly, 'would it upset you greatly if I married?'

'Married, Mr Macnamara?' Mrs Baxter had stuttered, growing crimson. 'I'm sure it's no business of mine *what* you do in that direction.'

A faint hope lingered, but was soon dispelled as the sheep-owner leaned coyly but purposefully forward. 'Ah yes, Mrs Baxter, but it is. For the question would then arise as to whether you, who are used to being in charge of your department here, would care for a young girl to take inevitable precedence'—and Julius had grinned knowingly at her, much to her vexation.

'A young girl, Mr Macnamara? So you're thinking of marrying a young girl?'

This was the intended cue for Julius to say who this young girl might be, but he had instantly become enigmatic. 'Just think it all over—think over what I say in its relation to your

25

own future,' he had told her—and dismissed her with a none too friendly wave.

The threat was evident: either she must accept this usurper (whoever she might be), or Julius would send her back to the city—with her fare paid, for sure, and possibly a month's wages, but certainly not a penny more. So sitting in her 'suite' (as she called it) on the least attractive side of the huge dwelling, Mrs Baxter pondered on who this young girl could be. And as she heard her employer driving off in his limousine to Cootamundra, she felt pretty sure the girl in question would be of the tennis party over there.

★

By now all the cars (and an occasional eccentric horse-drawn buggy) were converging down the hot tracks on Cootamundra. Sometimes they met up and formed convoys, with many a merry shout and helping of each other at the gates. Almost inevitably some vehicle would break down (for we are in the relatively early days of motor transport), and haulage would be arranged, or transfer of strapping giggling girls among the hatchet-eyed hard-buttocked boys who drove the racing motors. Clouds of orange dust rose upon the plains, and the white cockatoos climbed higher, screeching into the gleaming hardness of the dark midsummer sky.

Like a *diva* preparing herself for a gala operatic evening, Helen Bailey had retired a moment to rest before the fray began. The district expected her to be beautiful and serene; and these she wished also herself to be, despite the trepidation of her heart. So she would lie down and collect herself, and then for long weary hours be splendid even if it killed her.

There was a knock: and every time this happened, Helen still thought it would be Walter, even though it hadn't been for years. 'Oh, Maureen,' said Mrs Bailey as the girl came in. 'What can I do for you, my dear? Please move those things and do sit down.'

Maureen, already attired in tennis shorts and shirt and looking smashing ('No looks to speak of, but my God—what a figure,' said Tommy Mulligan to J G), sat astride a chair and gazed at Helen Bailey. 'It's what I can do for you,' she answered gravely.

Mrs Bailey looked a bit alarmed: she liked solicitude about herself, but not anxiety, since this aroused her own and punctured her hard-won calm. 'Do for me, dear?' she said a little sharply.

Maureen picked her words. 'I've had the feeling, Mrs Bailey,' she said almost severely, 'that you've been doing too much for all of us of late.' Maureen was frowning: due to the concentration needed when a young creature, for the first time, thinks of another and tries to put herself in this other's place.

'Too much for you? Oh, don't be silly!' said Helen Bailey doubtfully, defensively.

'Yes, Mrs Bailey. You're far too kind to us, and take all our little troubles on your shoulders. It must wear you out at times . . .'

Helen was touched—though aggravated by that 'wear you out'. But touched more than aggravated all the same. 'Let me give you a kiss, Maureen,' she said, 'and then we'll not think any more about all these things.'

Maureen gave her a frank warm kiss, such as later would delight her husband. A generous kiss, no peck, of the rare kind that leaves the giver exposed and vulnerable.

'It is true,' said Helen (who was strangely disturbed by this almost masculine embrace), 'that I get tired sometimes. I'm not so young as I was, for one thing'—and she flashed a sad, eager, slightly angry smile . . .

Here Maureen interrupted emphatically: 'Well, as to that, Mrs Bailey, all I can say is I hope I keep my looks later on like you have.'

'Oh, Maureen, you're so sweet! Here! I've got a little present for you. Of no value really, but just as a memento.'

She opened a drawer and took out an Australian opal (harbinger of ill fortune, did Maureen but know), unmounted and wrapped in cotton wool. The girl took it and unfolded it. It blinked at her insinuatingly.

'Gee, thanks, Mrs Bailey,' she said simply—for Maureen had that rare gift (far rarer than that of giving gracefully) of accepting a present without embarrassment or fuss.

She looked at Helen and enquired, 'Can I say something to you, Mrs Bailey? Something I really oughtn't to?'

Helen, foreseeing what it would be, twitched slightly and then nodded with a sweet reluctant smile.

Maureen chose her words carefully, like someone crossing a creek on stepping-stones. 'It's about you and Mr Bailey . . . Can I go on?'

'Yes, do go on, dear, do . . .'

'Well. I'm fond of you, Mrs Bailey, as I hope you know, and as a matter of fact I'm fond of your husband also, because he's always been nice to me in his way up here. Well, now, listen, please. One day I dare say I'll get married.' Maureen paused. 'So can you tell me, if you don't mind me asking, what went exactly wrong? Between you and he, I mean?' Maureen frowned, looking almost ugly, concentrating chiefly now on the problem insofar as it affected her young self.

Helen hesitated. She would have liked, in a way, to try to tell this young girl, if only to try to define to herself what *had* gone wrong. But this definition, though she had sometimes attempted it, was too hurtful to be borne—or rather, the truth it led to was. It was not that Helen, in her rare wounded moments of lucidity, did not know—or guess—what stood irrevocably between herself and Walter Bailey; but that what did, seemed to her so petty and so vulgar by comparison with the great dream of beauty in her soul! So squalid, sad and silly to begin with, but increasingly how tragical a folly! Philosophers tell us that to know ourselves is, in the end, the pathway if not to felicity, to resignation and acceptance. But Helen wanted neither to accept nor to resign: she wanted to be her own splendid vision of herself, even if at the hard cost of reality! And this, though so futile, was nevertheless Helen Bailey's particular kind of fortitude, of courage. She had blind faith if not wisdom, and accepted the price of her cherished illusion by her pain.

Perhaps, if Helen at that moment had tried to be franker—and confessed then what to no one else, not even to herself, she had ever dared fully to confess—the taut springs that locked her mind and heart might have eased and prepared the way for some kind of fulfilment. But to admit the source of her misfortunes to herself was far too cruel; and as for sharing her secret with this girl who, even though she liked and trusted her, might one day, perhaps unconsciously, betray her . . . So she decided on a half truth, and began, with a sly expression on her handsome face that Maureen detected and suddenly found a bit repulsive, 'Maureen, dear, tell me first. Are you . . . well are you what is called . . . ?'

'Am I what, Mrs Bailey? Go ahead . . .'

'Are you, Maureen—I know it's an old-fashioned word—are you what people call a virgin?'

Maureen was rather taken aback, but not excessively. 'Well, Mrs Bailey,' she said, 'as a matter of fact, I am. Not but what a boy or two hasn't tried to put a stop to that . . .'

'And you haven't let them?'

Maureen blushed and frowned again—not by embarrassment, but at the thought of the boy or two's effrontery. 'You see, Mrs Bailey,' she said slowly, 'I'm all for it, yes, but I believe in love.'

'And you haven't been in love yet?'

'As it happens, not yet, I haven't, no.'

Helen Bailey, turning nosey, shot off at a tangent, and even looked off at an angle as she spoke. 'Has Nancy had boys, Maureen, do you suppose?'

'Oh—her? Well, I'd say dozens.'

'Are you quite sure?'

'Sure I'm sure. She's told me so, anyway, and I've used my eyes . . .'

'And she doesn't . . . doesn't mock you because you haven't?'

'Nance? I'd not care if she did. We've got different ideas, we two, about what a heart-throb means . . .'

'I see . . .'

Maureen's curiosity, now thoroughly aroused, felt entitled, because of Helen's probings, to satisfy its original compulsion. 'So you and Mr Bailey, then . . . is it something of that nature that went wrong?'

Helen stammered slightly, and retreated even from a partial confession in her reply. 'Oh no, Maureen, it was nothing really of that nature . . . it's more a question of temperament, you see. My husband's difficult . . . perhaps I'm not all that easy either . . . so there are incompatibilities . . .'

Maureen, as it happened, didn't know what the word meant, let alone understand what Helen might possibly mean by it. And as for Helen, she had decided already this conversation had gone on long enough. Had she not woken from a light sleep when Maureen entered—and been in that state wherein dream merges for an instant into actuality—she would not have let this exchange take place at all. And now, well awake, she could not bring herself to confess a secret that seemed shameful and foolish to her, as well as her disaster! Nor, to her credit, did she wish to disabuse Maureen about sex, or love, or whatever both can combine to make, for this girl, she felt, would probably be more fortunate than she. 'I think I'll have my shower, now, dear,' she said, abruptly rising.

'But Mrs Bailey,' said Maureen, getting up too. 'Can't situations of that kind ever be remedied?'

Helen confronted her, looking at once bitter. 'Perhaps they can, dear—I really just don't know.'

'Well, I do hope they can,' said Maureen, thinking now not of herself, but once again of Mrs Bailey.

As is always the case when confidences are sought at a moment not yet propitious for them, deceit, hostility and rancour hovered momentarily in the air. They were standing apart by the double window, with its view over the kitchen garden, courts, and plain. Bending to pick loganberries, they observed a stranger: a boy in white tennis shorts and a T-shirt pulling down high boughs of the bush with his racket.

'He's got a cheek,' said Maureen, '—who is he?'

'A newcomer to the district, I expect,' said Helen, feeling herself suddenly as if in a trance.

'I dare say it's that kid Tommy Mulligan was bringing over, that Norman person. I'll go down and give him a ticking off.'

'Oh, but there's thousands of loganberries this year, despite the drought! There's thousands!' cried Helen Bailey, her eyes fixed on the marauding youth with fascination.

Maureen moved towards the door. 'No doubt there are,' she said, 'but he's come here for tennis, not to eat us out of house and home.'

*

'And what do you think you're up to?' said Maureen to the stranger.

Norman turned slowly round and looked at her. Most human creatures have been taught, or school themselves, by modesty as much as prudence, to mask the query in their gaze, and hide the thoughts that flash into their souls. But not so Norman Culley: his mind was devious, but his glance was frank. Without replying for a moment, he looked Maureen up and down: a blatant animal appraisal, and one that announced his determination to get his own way, if he could, without concession.

'And who might you be?' he answered. 'Are you one of Helen's two girls I've heard of?'

'Has Mrs Bailey said you can call her Helen?'

Norman smiled wickedly. 'She hasn't,' he said, 'but I bet you whatever you like she'll ask me to soon after we've met . . .'

Maureen, though convinced by his assurance, said, 'Son, you strike me as being a bit of a skite.'

'That's been said before about me, sister, and it doesn't worry me that much. Any man who knows his own mind, and knows what he wants, is called a skite. It's envy, you see—and jealousy means nothing to me.'

Now in his voice Maureen could detect a larrikin tone: and on this boy's stringy muscular shoulders she could discern large chips that gave her the advantage.

'Well, I'm Maureen,' she said, 'and we might as well be friends if you don't mind. Especially as you're partnering me in the first set according to the draw we made this morning.'

'Oh, I am, am I?' Norman emerged from the loganberry bushes, twirling his racket expertly and gently. 'Well, in that case we're going to *win*, Maureen,' he told her earnestly, 'and I do hope you're going to back me up. Because I *like* winning, and we're going to come out top, you and I, in the whole bloody tournament this afternoon.'

'They tell me you're hot stuff,' said Maureen, impressed by this youth despite herself.

'I am,' the boy answered, blinking a challenge.

'Well, you might as well come and have a lemon squash and meet the others.'

'Lemon squash?' Norman laughed unpleasantly. 'Don't you have any beer in this luxury establishment?'

'We do, but it won't improve your game, will it?'

32

'That's for me to decide—come on.' He tapped Maureen lightly on her bottom with his racket. 'Hands off the model, son,' she cautioned, and led the way over to the wide back veranda.

*

There Tommy Mulligan was having an interview with Nancy that he intended to be decisive. 'Now listen, Nance,' he said. 'Let's come straight up to the point. Which is as follows. As you well know, I'm quite a bit sweet on you.'

'I've guessed that, Tommy, and it's nice of you to be.'

'So,' said the engineer leaning seriously forward, 'why don't you and me get spliced?'

Nancy smiled, not unkindly. 'No, boy,' she said briskly. 'Not you and me.'

Tommy was doubly vexed, because when you come to the point with a girl the least you can expect is that she'll hesitate before refusing. 'Oh?' he said crossly, downing a drink. 'Can you give me sane reasons why you won't?'

Nancy contemplated him. How truthful to be? Not, certainly, so truthful that her words would exclude the possibility that, if all else failed, Tommy Mulligan would still dance her attendance. And yet Nancy respected Mulligan enough to tell him some of her real motives; besides which she was an outspoken girl, as much by native insolence and insensitivity as by candour.

'Tommy,' she said, 'there's certainly two reasons. One is I like you, but don't fancy you that way . . .'

'Wait a bit, Nance . . .'

'*You* wait a bit—you asked me . . . The other is, boy, I mean to marry money—just like that. And money to me means property which, as I happen to know, you haven't got.'

Evidently Tommy Mulligan regarded these as serious objections, for he did not take offence. Instead he said to her almost paternally, 'Well, Nance, to take the second first, I don't think you'll find the squatters' sons will look at you that way.'

'Oh no? You don't?'

'Oh no, I don't. They'll bed down with you, certainly, and I don't blame them. But up here, they're clans: sheep marrying sheep, I tell you.'

'Yes? What about Helen Bailey? She hadn't got a cent when she hooked old Walter.'

'Helen Bailey's a special case; and so for that matter's Walter.'

Nancy frowned. 'Well, you don't fancy my chances, but I do. I'm no fool, Tommy, and I know the boys up here—in fact, I think I know them better than you do, if only because I'm a woman.'

'So you're going to sell yourself.'

'Put it that way if you care to. But that doesn't mean, if the boy acted right, I wouldn't make a decent wife to him.'

'Got any particular boy in mind?'

Nancy looked inward. 'Several,' she said. 'And believe me, Tommy, I'll get one of them or bust.'

Tommy Mulligan sighed, then said to her, 'As for the first thing you mentioned, Nancy, I may not be all that glamorous, but I'd be steady. I may drink more than is good for me, but I'm the sort of man who when he makes his mind up . . . well, I stick around.'

'I'm sure you would, Tommy. But not for me.'

'You're much mistaken, Nance,' the engineer said gravely, with a slight point of vexation. 'You and I don't fit in up here, so we should team up together.'

Nancy gazed at him. 'I *mean* to fit in, Tommy. Just you watch my smoke.'

★

Julius Macnamara, having paid his respects to Mrs Bailey (and bestowed on her a flattery which, bordering on insolence, always embarrassed her), set out on a secret mission of his own: which was no less than to beard Walter Bailey in his lair, and 'have it out with him' on a (to Julius) highly important topic.

Julius knew full well that Walter Bailey would not at all want to see him, but knew equally that he could not, or would not, refuse to do so. For whatever their personal feelings about each other, the two most significant landowners in the district could never ignore entirely each other's presence, since their interests coincided at so many points—pastoral, political and even social.

Had Walter known of Julius's approach, he would have made himself scarce or feigned departure. But anticipating such manœuvres, Julius had spied out the land and spotted Walter through a bedroom window lying half naked on his bed and reading *Blackwood's Magazine*. A sharp tap on the panes, and the spuriously affable countenance of his neighbour, convinced Walter that reasonable escape would be impossible.

He opened the front door of the annexe, and admitted Julius to the masculine quiet of the cooler gun-room. He served him a whisky, and then sat down patiently to be thoroughly bored ... yet not altogether bored, since Julius never visited him without a purpose, and he was sufficiently curious to wonder what this might be.

Julius's approach, as he anticipated, was oblique. He talked first of the drought, and raised a red herring with which Walter was already long familiar. 'So once again, I ask myself, Walter' (he—and perhaps Helen—were the only persons in the district who used this first name) 'why you don't accept my long-standing offer of substantial irrigation.'

'We've been into all this before, Macnamara. The cost's too high, and I'd be completely dependent on you.'

'Oh come! It's technically feasible ... and think of the advantage it would be to me! If *you* came in, others would, and the cost of the pipe-lines and pumping-stations from the artesian bores would be proportionately reduced.'

Walter smiled without malice. 'I know you, Macnamara. You're a business man, not a pastoralist. You'd get us all in your clutches, and then try to buy us out.'

'Believe me, Walter, on that point you're entirely wrong. What use would I have of further land? I've got all I need, and my interests, as you must know, are increasingly in the capital.'

'Then what *is* your motive? Philanthropic?'

'Well, perhaps,' said Julius, lighting a cheroot (Walter was a non-smoker, and detested the odour), 'one might say my motives, in the present case, are twofold. In the first place, I don't mind admitting to you that I want to stand, next election, for the Assembly in this area. And if I have public works to my credit, that will surely assist in me in my candidacy.'

'Excellent! And what's the real motive?'

Here Julius rose, and paced the room a moment with portly gravity. Then turning on Walter Bailey, he said sternly: 'As you know, Walter, I am unmarried. Now—consider. Time advances: I am growing older. I have perhaps ten or twenty years of active life before me in which . . . well, to be frank, Walter, in which I could at last produce an heir.'

Walter was genuinely surprised. That Julius Macnamara was a 'confirmed bachelor' was a dogma in the district to which Walter had also always subscribed.

'And so?' said Walter with increasing caution, and a premonition of distaste.

Julius blinked, paused, stood still on tip-toe a moment, then said, 'I wish to ask Maureen if she will be my wife.'

'*Maureen?*'

You dirty old bastard, thought Walter. You obscene grotesque old idiotic goat. But a second thought immediately occurred to him. Maureen had no 'prospects', other than the possibility of marriage. That she could do better for herself—and would in any case reject this preposterous offer out of hand—Walter did not doubt a moment. But all the same, old Julius *was* rich, and the girl had the right to say 'no' for herself. (Or possibly 'yes'? For Walter, though he liked Maureen in a fairly remote sort of way, was highly mistrustful of the integrity of woman-kind.)

'I don't really see,' he answered at last, 'what this has to do with me.'

'You are, Walter, in a sense, this young girl's guardian.'

'She has family, you know, down south . . . in the fruit country, I believe . . .'

'No doubt she has: and I shall certainly approach them if Maureen were to look kindly on my suit. But meanwhile you will understand, Walter, it would scarcely be honourable on my part were I to approach the girl without first addressing myself, as I have done, to you.'

'Honourable', foresooth, thought Walter—you twisting old rogue. What are you up to, telling me all this? But he said, 'Have you mentioned this . . . project, at all, to Mrs Bailey?'

'Frankly—no. I deemed it should be discussed first man to man.'

Walter considered. 'Well, all I can say to you,' he told Julius at last, 'is that I think you'd better speak to the girl yourself.'

'Obviously. But . . . could you not perhaps prepare the ground for me a little?'

Walter frowned heavily. 'In what way?' he asked.

'In what way?' Julius smiled. 'Well, perhaps by pointing out to her that, despite an undoubted discrepancy in our ages, any marriage to me would have substantial material advantages.'

'No,' Walter said. 'She's not a fool, and she'll know that for herself without my telling her.' There was a silence, and then Walter added (not without malice) 'And what about Mrs Baxter?'

'Mrs Baxter,' said Julius, instantly and coldly, 'is my *house-*

keeper; and my relations with her—you may believe me or not, Walter, as you please—are of the utmost rectitude. In the event of my nuptials, she could go or stay as she, or others, best decided.'

'I suppose so,' said Walter. 'Well, thank you for telling me— though I'm bound to say I think it was unnecessary for you to do so.'

'Ah, as to that . . . well, I did perhaps have an additional motive in so doing, since another aspect of the matter had occurred to me . . .'

'Oh?' said Walter, instantly on his guard.

'Be patient with me, please, while I explain. I know you are a man of honour—that hardly needs saying—and not open to propositions which you might consider dubious. Nevertheless. In the event of Maureen's agreeing to my suit I would like to say I would view the matter of the irrigation of your station, Cootamundra, somewhat differently.'

'What does that mean, Macnamara?'

'Precisely this. Subject of course to your approval, I would consider irrigating Cootamundra without cost to you provided that—as I anticipate would be the case—other stations joined in the expense of the extension of the pipeline.'

Julius was playing a tricky card, and knew it. For Walter was proud, and pride can reject the most obvious material benefits! But Julius knew equally how attached Walter was to his ancestral acres, and how deeply he longed for them to bloom as only drenching water could make them do.

'You're trying,' said Walter slowly, 'to strike a bargain with me. I get free water if I use my influence on Maureen.'

Julius nodded, half anxious, half complacent, and said nothing.

'You're a cunning man, Macnamara,' Walter said at last, '—perhaps too cunning, really to succeed.'

Julius was still silent. 'You'd better see the girl,' Walter said 'and tell me what she answers.'

Julius nodded, bowed slightly, opened the wire netting of the flyproof door, and disappeared into the darkness of the sun. As soon as he had gone, Walter clenched his hands and muttered, 'I hope to God she has the good sense to reject him.'

*

Maureen, Nancy, Norman Culley and J G Eaton were sipping miscellaneous drinks beneath the monster peppercorn. 'So from what you tell us,' Nancy said, 'you're thinking of migrating north to Queensland.'

'That's about it,' said Norman. 'The frontiers are closed down here in the southern states. These people—' and he waved his racket round as if to comprise all the territories of the local squatters '—have moved in long ago and grabbed up everything. But up in the north, if you work like a Chinaman, the government will still allot you land . . .'

'What will you do on it?' asked Maureen.

'Grow sugar . . . tobacco . . . bananas . . . tropical crops and all that tack.'

'You know anything about all that?' said Nancy.

'Not yet, I don't. But I didn't know anything about tennis till I took it up and worked at it so I became junior champion of the state by the time I was sixteen.'

They were impressed by this; for a sporting achievement always convinces Australians—even their intellectuals and politicians.

'Margaret,' said J G, 'swears by the tropical north. She says she'll miss it badly when she comes down here to little old Victoria . . .'

No one was much interested by this thought. However, Nancy said, 'Couldn't you get a job up there, J G? Aren't there radio stations up in Queensland too?'

'There are, yes—but not for me, Nance, you know. After my

year on that Pacific Island, I've had enough of tropical surroundings . . .'

There was another silence, during which Maureen was all too aware that this forward, conceited boy was undressing her visually once again. 'Come on, J G,' she said, rising. 'Let's have a knock-up before lunch.'

'A pleasure, Maureen,' said the engineer, hoisting his stringy frame awkwardly from the deck-chair, and adjusting his concave spectacles. 'Any other volunteers?' he continued, beaming in a scout-masterly way.

The two others shook their heads, and J G and Maureen went off chattering down the track. 'I could do with that girl,' said Norman, as if to himself.

'You like her?' said Nancy. 'Well, she's no push-over, I can tell you that.'

Norman looked at Nancy narrowly and said evenly, 'What do you bet me I don't make it with her before the day is out?'

Nancy, affecting pudency, pouted; and she *was* a bit shocked —not by the boy's thought, but by its frank expression. Then she smiled. 'So you're feeling like that, are you?' she said. 'Well, all I can say is, it's not very complimentary to me.'

'Oh, you—you're all right, Nancy, I can see *that* . . . You and me could understand each other—I realized that the moment I set eyes on you. But fact is, I fancy this other sheila—she's so prim and proper. I know, Nance, you'll understand . . .' and he banged the strings of his racket lightly on her knee.

Nancy nodded, and did not appear to be offended. After a while she said, 'And this Margaret of J G's. What's she like, exactly?'

'What—her? Oh, just an ordinary sort of tart . . . you know— just a sheila like any other . . . Buck teeth, but juicy tits—you know the kind.'

'You seem,' said Nancy, 'to have very definite opinions about girls.'

Norman reflected. 'I'll tell you something, Nance. Girls are all right: they're necessary, and I take my hat off to the darlings. But this is a man's country and, by Gawd, the man's got to stay top dog.'

'I expect you're right,' said Nancy without irony. She rose, stood at her best advantage (which was considerable), and said, 'You care for a dip before we feed our faces?'

'A dip in what?'

'The big dam. It's half empty now, and there may be yabbies, but you can still splash around a bit in it . . .'

'Isn't it grubby?'

'You can have a shower after, if you don't use too much fresh water.'

'Okay—what about togs? I didn't bring any over.'

Nancy's eyes narrowed. 'Oh, there'll be nobody down there just now, I don't expect,' she said.

Norman grinned and followed her down the leaf-decked track among the gums. There were patches of purple shade, then shafts of hot sun like spot-lights, so that the walk down to the water was as if inside a kaleidoscope. The thick air was saturated with the sour pungent eucalyptus, bringing oily globules of sweat out on both their hot young skins. They emerged into a long paddock, where the orange banks of the oblong dam rose six feet of crumbling clay about the yellow flaccid water. It shimmered in the heat, but looked tepid and inviting.

Beside the dam, Nancy casually undressed. Norman glanced round, then did the same. By two piles of clothes, they contemplated each other. Nancy caught his eye.

'Well, which first?' she said. 'The swim or else the other?'

Norman didn't answer, but carrying his shorts, he took her moist hand and walked her slowly on the cracked clay to the far side of the dam. There hung in the air that concentration, and that electricity, which presage an unexpected sexual encounter; absolutely animal, devoid of any superfluous affection.

In a patch of shade beside tall bracken Norman said, 'Well this ought to do,' and throwing his shorts down on the ground he yanked Nancy heavily beside him.

★

Helen was being bored by Tommy Mulligan. The scene was the drawing-room, rarely used—except later on when the carpet would be pulled up for dancing—because everyone preferred the spacious shaded verandas that ran round three sides of the rambling house. But Helen liked this room, and was wont to receive in it if any one could be enticed there. For though its furnishings were of colonial elegance—leaning heavily on chintzes, and book-cases never opened, and a grand piano laden with aboriginal curios and draped with a Hong Kong shawl—it had a cool tranquillity which Helen prized. A bull, it is said, on entering the ring, will make instinctively for that portion of it where it feels safest and most at ease. And such a spot, in the big house at Cootamundra, was the faded grace of this saloon to Helen.

Tommy was boring Helen because he was telling her what she already knew: that he wanted to marry Nancy. And Helen— she was shrewd about others if unrealistic about herself—had long realized that Nancy's ambitions lay elsewhere. She regretted this, since she felt that—economically speaking, at all events—the couple was well matched, and she knew well that the potential mothers-in-law of the district were far, far tougher than Nancy perhaps yet realized. Also she liked Tommy Mulligan, who was one of the few men in the district who had never once, even accidentally, offended or humiliated her.

'Couldn't you say a word to Nancy, Helen?' said the love-lorn engineer in final desperation.

'Tommy, I would gladly, but to what purpose? I've really no influence over Nancy whatever: none, really, and she's a very decided kind of girl, even though I think nine times out of ten she's quite mistaken.'

'Well, I'll just have to keep on trying, I suppose.'

Helen nodded kindly, but said nothing: for she was awaiting a tactful moment to head the conversation in a more desirable direction.

'Tell me, Tommy,' she said suddenly. 'This boy Norman you brought over. He's closely related to J G?'

'Some sort of cousin, I believe . . . And to tell you the truth, Helen, I think poor old J G already regrets his presence.'

'Oh—why, Tommy? He seems a nice sort of a young fellow . . .'

'Well—take his escapade yesterday, for instance. Not that it wasn't partly my own silly damn fault, I must admit . . .'

Helen arched her brows.

'You see, we came back from the township a bit tanked up with grog. Well, that was all right, but then Norman Culley climbed a radio mast.'

'All the way up?' said Helen, turning to gaze through the window at the tall pylons on the distant horizon.

'Not only all the way up, but when he reached the platform where the cross-piece connects with the main mast, he walked right out to the far end of it.'

'Wasn't that extremely dangerous?'

'You bet it was. Apart from which, if the Chief Engineer had spotted him, either I or J G or the both of us might have got the order of the boot—and pronto.'

'And he got down safely?'

'Came down cool as cucumber. Christ, did I give the silly yob a ticking off! But it seemed to have no effect whatever on him.'

'He's a wilful boy, then,' said Helen ruminatively.

'He's a brash young idiot. And I tell you, Helen, the sooner he leaves the district—well, the better I'll be pleased.'

Helen nodded, then said to him, 'All the same, Tommy, as I

haven't met him yet—and I do like to see all the guests, you know, especially strangers, soon after they arrive—do you think you could hunt him out and bring him here and introduce him?'

'Why, of course, Helen. I didn't know you hadn't seen him yet. The kid's got no manners, just like I told you.'

'Oh,' said Helen a little wistfully, 'I *saw* him a moment, but I haven't *spoken* to him as I'd like to, Tommy . . .'

★

Down by the courts, Julius Macnamara, watching Maureen and J G Eaton bashing the ball about, was plotting how he could get rid, for a moment, of the engineer. The tennis, moreover, bored him, and was indeed a ludicrous spectacle. For J G was one of those non-players who expend tremendous energy for scant results. If vim, gusto and utter commitment had won laurels, J G would have been champion of Australia. But as it was, his frenetic vigour—coupled with the myopia of his eyes—gave most points to Maureen without her having to struggle much to earn them.

Julius, ever resourceful, hit upon a stratagem. 'I wonder, J G,' he said affably, as the engineer subsided a moment in exhaustion by the summer-house, 'if I could prevail on you to fetch me a cooling drink? I'd go myself, of course, but to tell you the whole truth, at my age the flesh is willing but the spirit, in this heat, just does wilt a little.'

The gallant engineer hastened to comply, and disappeared up the track towards the house, slashing at the golden wattles with his racquet.

Maureen, who had no particular wish to consort solo with Mr Macnamara, continued slamming balls accurately across the net till Julius rose and, beckoning to the summer-house, said, 'Do come and chat a while with an old codger, dear young lady.'

'Oh, you're not all that old, are you?' she said politely—and

44

vaguely, for to Maureen anyone over twenty-three was no longer young at all.

'Well, you might say,' rejoined Julius, 'there's life in the old dog yet . . . I've looked after myself, Maureen—I always pay particular attention to my health . . . and beauty (ha, ha, ha).'

There are remarks which contain hints of other meanings and which, like wedges, are intended to prize open situations usually left obscure. Maureen scented this in Julius's innocent observation, and was instantly upon her guard.

'Well, I'm glad to hear your health's good, Mr Macnamara.'

'Maureen,' said Julius avuncularly. 'We've known each other quite a while now, so don't you think you could drop the "Mr" and call me simply Julius?'

She gazed at him. 'Julius? Well, to tell you the truth, Mr Macnamara, it's always struck me as a rather comical kind of a name.'

'Oh, has it?' said the landowner, a point of malice darting in his eyes. 'Well, Maureen, evidently the first of the Caesars didn't think so.'

Maureen said nothing. The first of the Caesars held no interest to her whatsoever. The last of the young Australians, however, was already much in her mind.

Somewhat non-plussed by this girl's capacity for silence without embarrassment or offensive intent, Julius girded up his intellectual loins, and tried again.

'Maureen,' he said, 'you're from the apple country, I believe.' (To say, in the district, 'the apple country' is the equivalent, in a city, of saying 'the wrong side of the tracks'. But Julius had carefully purged his tone of all contempt.)

'Apples, plums, peaches, nectarines, apricots—all that sort of tack,' she said with a trace of boredom.

'So your parents have . . . substantial means?' he asked (knowing full well, from the state of the fruit market, that they certainly hadn't).

'Old Mum and Dad? Well, they depend on the co-operative, and also on world markets, according to what Dad says. And that usually seems to mean they get poor prices.'

'Yes,' Julius replied—infusing into this basic monosyllable a wealth of imputation.

'On the other hand,' said Maureen, sensing her childhood slighted and leaping to its defence, 'it's a fine life because, as Dad so often says, there's more instrinsic value in a case of apples than in a whole bale of fleeces . . .'

Julius smiled tolerantly. 'Value? Yes, but what value?'

'To your health is what he means, I reckon.'

'Ah—to your health. But health, my dear child, is not everything, even though it's a lot. And that leads me to the notion,' he now went on, 'as to whether you, Maureen, have given as much thought to your future as a wise girl certainly ought to do.'

'My future, Mr Macnamara?'

Nothing's more irritating—or frustrating—than to have your observations echoed back as questions. 'Yes, your future, Maureen,' he said almost severely.

When those older than the young make categorical statements about these young people's destinies, the young, even though justly suspicious, are nevertheless impressed because they rightly sense their own painful ignorance on so many matters. 'Oh, I don't think much about the future,' Maureen said dubiously. 'Life's all right to me here just as it is now.'

'Ah, but is it?' Here Julius contrived to look almost like a (possibly unfrocked) bishop. 'A young girl, Maureen, particularly if not of what I might call substantial means, ought certainly to ponder a moment on her destiny. For example: let me be frank: what future is there here for you at Cootamundra?'

Confronted with this question, which she had always declined to consider, Maureen saw dimly there was none, or little. 'They say the future takes care of itself,' she answered.

'On that,' said Julius decisively, 'I can assure you that it does not. It has to be planned, or else it simply ceases to exist! No, Maureen dear. The future is a matter of sensibly weighing up the pros and cons and various alternative possibilities.'

Somewhat blinded by this science, though still feeling remote from all his verbiage, Maureen waited for the pastoralist to continue.

'Let me be frank,' said Julius, 'and let us try to be helpful to each other. First, then, let us consider yourself. The possible alternatives awaiting you' (he placed a finger on the first of three stubby digits), 'are spinsterhood—in which, dear, we surely cannot believe—a poor marriage for what's called love, or . . . a richer marriage in which the element of affection would be created by the happy passing of the years.'

'What's wrong,' Maureen said, 'with love and money?'

'Oh, as to that . . .' Julius's rotund face, when an ironical expression was planted on it, appeared positively distorted, '. . . it rarely happens in this world, you know: I mean if, as in your case, my dear, the girl is—to be candid—poor.'

Till the moment she heard these words, Maureen had never considered herself to be 'poor'. She knew she had no money, but that did not make her *poor*. Yet it dawned on her now unpleasantly that, for some future date, Julius might very well be right.

'So what are you saying, Mr Macnamara, that you think I ought to do?'

'A sensible question, Maureen dear, and I'll give you a straight and sensible answer from the fund of my experience. But first another question: are you in love with anybody now?'

'In love? Well, no—not exactly.'

'Love, it is true, can sustain against material misfortune, if only for a while and even then, I'd say, among the very young. Therefore, had you told me that your heart was already committed—and that even to some penniless boy or other—I would have said, "By all means, Maureen! Challenge fortune in the name of joy!"' Julius raised his eyes a moment to the hot heavens. 'But since, as you tell me, you are fancy-free at present,' he continued, 'why not consider my third reasonable alternative, which is to secure your material welfare for all time even if love, in its more superficial sense, may at first seem to be absent?'

Maureen got the gist of this, though she was considerably puzzled; and also beginning to think old Julius was (if not drunk) a nosey-parker taking something of a liberty.

'So what are you saying I should do?' she asked again.

Julius leaned forward and said softly (in tones intended to be reassuring and paternal . . . and yet decorously erotic), 'Do? You should marry me, my dear.'

'You?' Maureen stared at him in incredulous amazement—so frank and unguarded a stare that even Julius was momentarily embarrassed. '*You*, Mr Macnamara?' she repeated.

'And why not?' cried Julius swiftly leaping into the supposed breach, and his craft mastering instantly his resentment. 'For I can offer you three things few others can: wealth and position, a faithful and affectionate heart, and then . . .' (she continued to gaze at him interrogatively) '. . . and then, well, obviously you will outlive me. If I died, Maureen dear, you could marry again, as a rich woman, whoever you chose to in the district.'

Come to think of it, from Julius's point of view it might seem a generous offer, however otherwise revolting. But it was neither the generosity nor even the incongruity that now most struck Maureen. What struck her was that this proposal was in a slight sense flattering, but in a much larger one, infinitely comical. For Maureen reacted to Julius's words immediately with her body. And looking at his—flabby though energetic in its hanging shantung suit—the notion of being associated intimately with *that* seemed to her grotesque in the extreme. If Julius had offered her wealth without commitment—offered to make her his heiress, say, or even to adopt her—how delightful! If he had even declared a love for her, she might have been touched, however much repelled. But Maureen was a country girl, and knew what marriage meant. And as to being *wife* to Julius Macnamara on these terms . . . why! she'd prefer J G Eaton even, or Walter Bailey! What a cheek! The fat old disgusting bastard! And having reached this point in her swift sequence of ideas, Maureen rose, looked at the landowner, and abruptly burst out laughing.

'You're a card, Mr Macnamara!' she cried out. 'You're a real old kidder, and you should be ashamed of yourself!'

Julius also rose, snatching about him, as older people do in the presence of the humiliating young, the dignified apparel of a tarnished seniority. Craft told him to say, 'Well, my dear, do think over what I've had to say,' or words to that effect soothing to his vanity, and keeping the door open to the possible consummation of his wishes. But the sight of Maureen's frank face and grin and sparkling mockery were too much for him. So he said in measured tones, into which a fair dose of venom was injected: 'Wisdom was never born of conceit, Maureen. You may live to regret an attitude I can only describe as cruel and improvident.'

But Maureen was not interested in Julius's wisdom; for she believed only in the wisdom of her own young body.

*

Summoned by Tommy to the presence of Helen Bailey, Norman Culley paused in the dim hall to examine himself in an ornate mirror. A faint fear existed in his mind that Helen, by some mischance, should have learned of his dallying with Nancy beside the dam—though he thought this improbable, even though Mulligan had met them on the pathway and given them a markedly peculiar stare before delivering Helen's message. No, what really perturbed Norman was that though he was prepared to be unimpressed by the local notabilities—and defy them with his larrikin malice if they tried to 'put upon' him—the legend of

Helen as the *grande dame* of the district had already reached him and, despite himself, impressed him. He sensed that Helen would not bully him, but genuinely dazzle; and this was the only kind of pressure Norman's defensive obstinacy found it difficult to withstand.

Satisfied with his appearance (and the removal of all apparent traces of the idyll), Norman knocked and entered, to find Helen playing the piano; and not playing Charlestons or Black Bottoms, but a piece that was evidently 'classical'. Now, everyone in the district loathed classical music, yet everybody was impressed by it—or rather, by anybody that could play it, for no one would invest in classical gramophone records or pianola rolls except, perhaps, in the former case, through patriotism, in the productions of Dame Nellie Melba—so that Helen's performances had a certain exotic rarity value, even if they didn't exactly give their occasional hearers any pleasure.

She heard him at the door, turned and smiled, yet continued playing—not, in truth, to try to beguile the lad, but because Helen respected the composer's intention enough to continue with him to the end. Norman stood by the never-used fireplace (for in winter they all retreated to the smaller, cosier 'parlour') and, encouraged by an amity emanating from Helen's graceful back, he boldly lit a cigarette. The piece was fortunately short (it was by Claude Debussy), and soon she rose to shake hands with her young visitor.

'Do sit down, Norman,' she said. 'And would you like a drink of some kind before lunch? I do hope you're not ravenous, but I'm sure the girls will soon have it all ready.'

('Not if old Nance has got anything to do with it,' Norman thought) but said, 'Well, I'd like a beer if you've no objection, Mrs Bailey.'

'Over there in the ice-chest: please just help yourself.'

Norman noted, with approval, that his hostess made no reference to his precocious affection for the bottle.

'What was that,' the boy asked, 'you were strumming just now on the goanna?'

'A French piece,' she answered. 'I was made to learn dozens when I was young, and it's just as well, for I'm far too idle these days ever to learn new ones.'

'As a matter of fact,' said Norman, rapidly gaining confidence, 'I can play by ear a fair bit myself, but not exactly the kind of number you were indulging in.'

'Ragtime and such?'

'Yes, that sort of tack. I hope you don't think them vulgar or too brutal . . .' the boy darted a swift glance of suspicion at the lady.

'Not a bit, I'm just envious. But I can't get the rhythm right—I suppose it's not of my generation.'

Norman nodded. 'You have to be your age,' he said, with no intended malice.

'Ah, yes!' Helen clasped her hands. 'And what is so funny about growing older, Norman, is that, believe me, you just don't feel it! It's absurd! I suppose it's even undignified. But as the years creep by—well, it's almost as if you felt the whole world ageing but you yourself just standing still!'

Norman looked at her levelly. 'You'd be thirty-eight or thereabouts,' he said.

Helen started slightly, but then smiled. '*That* is a woman's secret,' she replied. 'And you, I'd say . . . well, I know, as a matter of fact—you're twenty-two.'

'Yes, hitting twenty-three,' he said. 'It's time I pulled up stakes and started moving.'

'Moving? You're going to leave our state, then?'

'I meant in a general way. But as a matter of fact, yes, Mrs Bailey, I'm heading it up to Queensland as soon as the cold weather comes down here.'

'Oh, what a pity! I mean for us!'

The ejaculation was spontaneous, and did not seem to surprise

Norman. Of course anyone who appreciated him would be sorry to see him go!

'But you're a city boy, Norman—from the city, like I am,' she added, to soften any suggestion of rural superiority. 'And how will you manage up in Queensland without the country experience?'

'I shall learn. You can learn anything you want to if you've got brains and muscles, Mrs Bailey.'

Helen smiled benevolently. 'How right you are, Norman dear, in what you say! And by the way, don't you think if I'm to call you "Norman", you should stop calling me "Mrs Bailey"?'

'It's to be Helen, then? Okay, Helen, I appreciate the privilege.'

There was a silence, as invisible physical antennae reached out between this ill-assorted pair. Helen broke it. 'Down there in the capital,' she said, 'a child often has a hard life—well, I know I did, anyway. And what about you, Norman? I don't suppose you had it all that easy—I expect you had to make your own way, didn't you?'

Norman looked suddenly venomous. 'No, as to that, I certainly did not have it easy,' he said in tones which, momentarily, directed the malice of recollection against Helen.

'You'd rather not talk of it?' she said, sensing the danger.

'On the whole, no—it's best forgotten. But I will tell you this. My dad and mum are both, in their way, good people. But they didn't care much for each other, so she had her men and he had his women on the side. Well, no objection to that on my part, if it hadn't have been I became like the tennis ball they bashed back and forward at each other. They *used* me, Mrs Bailey—oh, it's Helen, isn't it, so sorry' (and Norman suddenly gave an astonishing, unexpectedly sweet smile)—'they *used* me in their battles with each other. And that's a thing I won't forgive, and don't mean to let ever happen to me again.'

His face had darkened, and Helen was impressed by his male

vehemence—and felt, also, no doubt, the kinship of one neurotic to another; for there are neuroses which, not conflicting, can match up and almost neutralize each other, leading to cordiality.

'Well, as for tennis balls,' she said, 'and battles, you must be at your best form this afternoon. And for that, what's needed is some food inside you, which I'm sure will be almost ready now . . .'

She rose; and Norman, who was not schooled to get up when a woman did, found himself automatically rising too.

'You're partnering Maureen to begin with, so I hear,' said Helen. 'You'll find if she's not brilliant, she's steady as a rock . . .'

'Oh, I know Maureen . . . She's all right, quite a decent sort of sheila . . .'

'You like her?' asked Helen Bailey, a slight tremolo vibrating in her voice.

'Maureen? Sure! She's a pearla sort of kid, I'd say. Bit young, of course, and cocky, but quite a beaut.'

'And . . . Nancy?'

Norman searched Helen Bailey's eyes, then smiled. 'Well, Nance is a girl and a half, it seems. Full of beans and Kruschen salts, if you understand what I mean.'

Helen thought she did, and was reassured. Then abruptly approaching Norman, who was standing two feet from her and a head and a half taller, she placed her hands lightly on his shoulders and gave him a swift kiss on his brow.

'There!' she said, releasing him quickly as if fearing a reaction only part of her desired. 'I do hope you'll be happy at Cootamundra, Norman dear.'

*

By now the company (save for those lingering at the hostelry in the adjacent township) had gathered in force and greed at Cootamundra. From an enormous central buffet, four trestle tables long, in the centre of the coolest veranda facing on the courts and far off radio station, there were dispensed to the guests mountains of food and gallons of beer from dishes and flagons under which the laden trestles creaked. The only concession Cootamundra made to the torrid climate was that the food was cold (even if the beer was warm). But otherwise, as befitted this land of present plenty and of initial poverty, whose original settlers had come from freezing zones, there was far too much to eat and drink for stomachs whose owners would soon be slamming balls about at a temperature approaching 90° in the shade.

From the guzzlers there arose what can only be described as a perpetual male roar punctuated by a staccato female screech. The atmosphere was amicable in the extreme—for what have neighbours to fear who know one another inside out, have identical agricultural problems, support the Country Party in politics and hate the banks—and even more the cities which battened on their labour . . . but whither, nevertheless, they longed to go on holidays? As is the Australian custom, the men soon drifted together and if they addressed the women, were matey to them as if they were males of a different sub-species; for though this country is uninhibited about sex, it has no conception of sexual mystery, glamour or romance.

And yet, these people *were* in a sense glamorous. They had a vigour, a physical perfection, a confidence, a youthful hope despite their cynicism, that have vanished from the ancient world. At rare moments in history, by a series of accidents never to be repeated, there flower societies in which the cult of *happiness* is paramount: hedonistic, mindless, intent upon the glorious physical instant! And such a benison had fallen, for a decade or so (and despite the recently remembered horrors of Gallipoli and of Ypres), on this generation protected by the seemingly fixed radiance of the kind sun and the nocturnal brilliance of the Southern Cross.

Gossip and chatter, unless you were in the know, might seem excruciatingly dull: confined as it was to local matters, mostly agricultural or comical or scandalous, with never a questing abstract notion to disturb this animal well-being. But to the locals this converse held the interest of a high debate in the Athenian agora, and if some Pallas Athene were required to bestow an ultimate grace on the proceedings, this role was filled to perfection by Helen Bailey: not eating much herself (and drinking nothing), passing from group to group radiating re-assurance, and yet (by some process known only to herself) never stemming the flow of ready conversation by her presence. And as she approached each group, its emotional temperature rose slightly; and as she departed from it, the warmth waned just as much, and they regretted her.

Also circulating, because he belonged everywhere and no-where, and had no intimates yet was on back-slapping terms with everyone, came Julius Macnamara. To register bonhomie, to be vociferously welcomed, was now a prime necessity to Julius. For Maureen's rebuff had hurt him, and when Julius was hurt (which was infrequently, since he arranged his existence so as not to be), he grew vindictive. But to be vindictive openly in the district would be fatal: hearts must be worn on sleeves up there, and *joie de vivre* perpetually registered. So to mask the searing of his vanity, Julius became even more pally than he was habitually —thumping backs, poking bellies, and bestowing on sweaty female foreheads, hands, and even necks a shower of moistened kisses.

A man like Julius knows the world well enough to understand a young girl may reject an old, if wealthy, suitor. True, calcu-lating rationally, he had supposed the riches of Macnamara's might outweigh, in Maureen's mind, a natural objection to his person. But his mistaken judgement proceeded really from an even deeper error. All realists have their flaws, and Julius's was that of imagination: ingenuity he possessed, and even devious

55

invention, but no fund of genuine inspiration. And thus, brooding for long over the thought of purchasing Maureen (for the plan had come to him ever since he had first seen her), he had so ruminated on this project obsessively in solitude, that Maureen had become, to him, no longer herself, but an extension of his own ego. He wanted her so much—and the idea of having her—that he had ceased to believe that this would be impossible. And when she had refused him, the Maureen of his daydreams had abruptly disappeared and been replaced by a hard, detestable girl who was a stranger and an enemy.

But would she perhaps, after reflection, change her mind? Julius, remembering her shocked and amused eyes, winced, and didn't think so. And by God, even if she *did*, she'd find she'd missed her opportunity! 'I am not to be refused!' cried Julius Macnamara to himself. 'I do not often ask, but when I do, I, Julius, am not to be denied! This girl has rejected *me*; and anyone who dares to do that deserves punishment!' So as he, too, moved from group to group, the shrillness of his chuckles and his sallies reflected the rising rancour in his heart.

If Julius, like Helen, was well received by each little phalanx of the guzzling horde, the reason was entirely different: for the fact was, they were rather afraid of Julius Macnamara. Australians, as is well known, fear no man in open battle; but in a battle of wits and of possessions, they well may. For Julius had so many fingers in so many local pies that almost every landowner owed him money—or owed it to someone else who did, which was perhaps even more disturbing. And so, even the most insensitive could detect, in Julius's candid exchanges, a threat, an undertone of unforgiving malice. But because Julius was rich, and because he had always taken care never to strike openly, the legend had arisen—intended to mask their own inner anxieties and preserve the myth that everyone in the district was a decent fellow—that Julius was, even if a bit far-fetched, and even if perhaps something of a menace, nevertheless almost certainly a *character*: 'old Julius', whom you welcomed effusively, and were as glad to see the back of.

When at one point in their peregrinations Julius came face to face with Helen Bailey, a thought entered the deft mind of the landowner. Walter Bailey, he was certain, would keep silence over the revelation of his intentions towards Maureen. But would Maureen herself? Almost certainly not (and here he was quite wrong)! So would it not be best, to anticipate the mockery that might descend on him should the district learn his suit had been declined, to first himself reveal it, on his own terms, to the lynch-pin of their little society?

'Helen, my dear,' he cried, 'a toast to you! Each Saturday at Cootamundra is, I declare, more delightful than the last! And what is the secret of this beatitude? It is you, Helen, the un-crowned queen of our community!'

Used to this sort of tone from Julius—in which each over-laden compliment hovered on the verge of an impertinence—Helen merely smiled at him and sank into a wicker chair.

'Ah me,' he continued, 'my only thought, on a glorious day like this, is "Would that I were younger!" Ah yes—would that I were young again!' Julius's eyes narrowed. 'And were I younger, Helen, do you know what I might do? Yes, even I?'

Helen raised her brows, her smile glued to her countenance.

'Why,' Julius cried, rising on tip-toe, 'why—I would carry off one of these young maidens!' And he waved his ringed hand at the galaxy of leggy, small-breasted Aussie beauties on the veranda. 'Yes—carry off Nancy! Carry off Maureen!'

Helen sipped an iced lime-juice cordial. 'You'd have to ask them first,' she said, with a glint of malice. 'They're strong young girls to carry off . . .'

'And that,' cried Julius in triumph, 'is precisely what I've done!'

Helen looked a bit startled. 'Are you serious?' she asked.

'As can be, Helen, as can be,' cried Julius with that smirking grin which announces the coming of a pleasantry. 'In a moment of fantasy—and out of pure devilment just to tease the girl—I fell on my knees beside the tennis courts and proposed my suit to young Maureen!'

Helen's expression clearly conveyed she did not consider Julius's account amusing. Not only because she did not wish the girls—or any woman, for that matter—to be slighted, even in an ill-considered jest (for marriage seemed to Helen a dreadfully grave matter), but as much because she did not like hearing, for the second time that day, that the two girls were being pursued by suitors.

'I hope you didn't upset her,' she said, with a sharpness unusual on her angelic lips.

'But of course not, dear Helen! Young Maureen entered into the spirit of the thing and rejected my mock offer out of hand, as I expected!'

Helen did not quite believe this version, but equally did not wish to pursue so muddlesome a topic. 'Maureen is a serious girl,' she answered vaguely, 'and I like her for it.'

Julius accepted this as answering sufficiently his intention of masking the truth, and turned to gaze at the subject of their conversation. She and Nance, waving chicken bones, were chattering with the trio from the radio station. They were so free with each other, so easy and casual in their exchanges, that Julius felt the suffering of those who are, by some defect of character or nature, excluded from communion with their fellow creatures. And as he saw Maureen laugh at something silly J G said, he felt towards her a great bitterness, not now so much on account of her refusal as because she dared (with nothing to her name!) to be so indifferently happy. It was intolerable he could make no impression on this girl's stupid felicity: and he there and then determined that he would. And slightly shifting his questing envious glance from Maureen to the sleasier and more lackadaisical Nancy, he wondered if the way to hurt the one girl might not perhaps be through the other.

Across the passion-fruit plantation, almost out of view, Walter Bailey could hear the festive din that, muted as it was by the hot wind, drifted in incoherent spasms from the house. He went to a cupboard, opened it, and from its top shelf took a racquet from among many that lay there higgledy-piggledy, among silver cups tarnished and fallen sideways, separated from their mock-marble bases. He made several strokes around the room, then undressed, had a short cold shower, changed into tennis flannels and taking a net bag filled with ancient balls, emerged from his annexe like a wombat from its lair. After a swift glance round about, he strode steadily in springing paces down towards the wind-hit courts.

★

Maureen knew, at the alfresco luncheon, that Norman would soon ask her to go off alone with him. And sure enough, after a meaningful glance or two, at a moment when most figures, extended on deck-chairs and lie-lows in post-prandial torpor, were snatching a short siesta before the battles of the afternoon, Norman rose, took Maureen by the arm, and said, 'What about, if we're going to play together, we have a knock-up just to get used to each other's style of action?' Maureen nodded, and the pair set off into the peak sun of the waning noon.

As soon as you emerged from the cool of the back veranda, the heat hit you: woof! You had practically to push your way through it, it was like a curtain of invisible warm cotton wool. Insects sung high, the earth steamed, and the distances were lost in haze. There was also, at moments, heavy silence, as if the country were shocked by the glare into a wounded pain.

Maureen walked behind Norman, and admired his figure: she didn't mind admitting it. For Norman, though his best friend couldn't call him handsome, was a lithe, springy, watchful eager joker, poised on each step like a puma on patrol: a vulnerable

lad, perhaps, but constantly prepared to lash back if affronted—
and even, Maureen felt, reliable in the defence of what was dear
to him . . . supposing, that is, to this vagrant kid, anything apart
from himself could be so. As for Norman, he was well aware of
this smashing haughty sheila walking behind him, and that her
silence betrayed a preoccupation with his person and his
presence. And as they passed under the gold sticky shadows of
the wattles he halted abruptly a moment, by intention, so that
she almost collided in the warm yellow gloom, and put a hand
out to rest upon his sweating shoulder. 'I thought I saw a snake,'
he said turning with a frankly deceitful smile.

'We do have them,' Maureen answered, 'but not often so near
the homestead . . .'

'Over there inside that bracken,' Norman said, pointing with
his racket. 'Shall I go and have a look and dig him out?'

'Why bother? They don't trouble you unless you step on
them . . .'

'Too true, they don't,' Norman said, showing however no
inclination to move on. He stared at Maureen and the girl's
frank cool gaze made him suddenly unsure and, unusually for
him, embarrassed. But gathering courage (aided by a tincture of
resentment that this girl managed to impress him), he said, 'Sit
down on that log awhile and I'll just go have a look.'

He simulated rummaging for the reptile, Maureen watching
his lithe darting movements, then he straightened up, returned
and stood up close to her, swinging his racket, so that his shorts
were about two feet from her face. She managed to hold his eyes
while he said nothing, swaying slightly before her seated body:
then abruptly he rubbed the sweat off his forehead with a bare
arm, cried, 'Well, come on, then, we'll dodge the old serpent,'
and taking Maureen's hand pulled her firmly to her feet and
dragged her after him towards the courts.

Coming out into the open, they suddenly saw and heard
Walter Bailey. He was standing on the far base line, practising

services with enormous vehemence, and these were indeed something to behold. For against his imaginary opponent, Walter slammed down volleys that skimmed narrowly across the net, struck the inside of the far base line with electric speed, and shot off at a long low angle which, Norman reflected, would be damn difficult to scoop up at all, let alone lam back. 'That's something!' he said to Maureen, whose hot wet hand he had not hitherto released.

But now she withdrew it. 'Mr Bailey,' she said, 'used to be a champion, so the story goes.'

'He still is, I reckon. Will he mind if we put in an appearance?'

'I don't think he will—let's try, anyway.'

Walter observed them, glowered quickly, but seeing they were alone, broke into an unusually sheepish grimace. Beckoning Norman, Maureen advanced resolutely, sure of her capital of credit with Mr Bailey, and striding down the court, presented her companion to his as yet invisible host. 'Mr Bailey,' she said, 'this is Norman Culley, from the radio, who's a bit of a champion too in his way, though I've no doubt you'd easily lick him hollow.'

The men shook hands, and Walter looked at the boy appraisingly. 'I wouldn't mind a game with you, Mr Bailey,' Norman said. 'For I believe though I'm younger than you are, you can teach me a trick or two.'

Walter nodded, and waved Norman with his racket towards the far end of the court. Maureen walked round collecting balls, and flung them expertly, half each towards the two opponents.

Norman crouched, waiting, as Walter took service, and he had decided to miss the first few both to flatter the old boy and discover what his line of play might be. He had resolved his best tactic was to force Walter off that base line, and make the old fellow run a bit, and tire him, if this were possible. Maureen was disappointed at his apparent initial incompetence, though glad for Walter Bailey that he was aceing this attractive young upstart so effectively. Then Norman, squeezing his eyes, and baring his big teeth, and squatting with ungainly tension (for though so effective, he was far from being a stylish player)—and having taken the measure of Walter's delivery and decided, even before the next serve came, how now to deal with it effectively—sent back a return or two high into the sky so that Walter, though he had the wind behind him, was now forced to raise his eyes into the sun. And though Walter smashed back low and viciously, Norman contrived to ladle up returns delivered at angles that had Walter, as he hoped, running to and fro like a hare. But here he had underestimated Walter Bailey. For the 'old boy' disclosed a remarkable turn of speed and, adopting Norman's stratagem, soon got the boy chasing helter-skelter. 'Right, you old bastard,' Norman thought—and proceeded to pull the ace out of his short-sleeved shirt: which was, with his height and his agility (for Norman, even in those days, could jump 6 feet $1\frac{1}{2}$ inches), to take his stand near the net and smash back *at* Walter—near as he could get it, the ball between the eyes. For Norman did not believe in 'sportsmanship'—my oath, he didn't; Norman believed in winning by any tactic barely permissible in the book.

Walter was not dismayed by this technique, though he found it distasteful, particularly in one so young who didn't really need to use it. But what did dismay him was that his eyes, behind beaded steel-rimmed spectacles, were not as eagle-sharp as they once were, so that he simply could not see these balls that sped at him. 'He's a bastard,' Maureen thought of her new young friend. 'He's a proper tyke and a coward, and I don't trust him a centimetre.'

A shot that actually hit Walter in a crucial spot (with a smack like a gun going off at distance) brought this friendly knock-up to an abrupt close. For Norman, full of solicitude, had leapt over the net to succour his opponent, and Walter resented this cruel youth's spurious attentions more than his actual wound. He backed from the boy and, holding his racket as if he might very well lash it across the lad's dishonest countenance, he said coldly, 'Well, you got what you wanted: my congratulations.'

'I hope I wasn't too hasty for you, sir,' said Norman, who never said 'sir' to anyone without malicious intent.

'You were just too effective,' Walter answered, and without another word—and only a brief nod to Maureen—he paced rapidly from the asphalt battlefield.

Maureen waited till he was out of view, then faced Norman levelly and said to him, 'Well, as for you, son, you're a right crook kid, and I hope you're pleased with yourself.'

'You think I am?' said the unrepentant victor.

'You had no need,' she answered, 'to humiliate him.'

'In my book,' said Norman, 'it's the best man who wins, no matter how. And as for humiliation, I can tell you no one has ever minded about humiliating *me*.'

He had come closer to Maureen, and now glared at her above their two dark stumpy mingling shadows.

'We don't play like that up here,' she said, conceding nothing.

'Oh, don't we? Not like *that* up *here*? Well, suppose we set about altering the rules and regulations?'

Fast and deliberately he grabbed Maureen, enfolded her in two taut arms, and kissed her as if he were eating a considerable lamb chop. She remained motionless until he desisted for a moment to judge of the effect on her: then she wrenched free and clouted him with her racket across the brain with a whack that resounded round the tennis courts and echoed in the gums.

★

Over at Macnamara's, Mrs Baxter was growing anxious and distressed. Julius was up to something, that was certain, and up to something more disturbing than ever before. Yet what hold could she have over him, the all-powerful Julius, and by what decisive bid could she frustrate his suspected plans? Mrs Baxter thought she knew the answer, and decided on a last and desperate throw.

So before her three-piece mirror, arranged as if in a stage dressing-room, she made herself up in that exaggerated way which was her pride—since it showed the opulent local rustics that, unlike them, *she* was vested with the glamour of things theatrical . . . but which style was equally the embarrassment of the district when they saw her because people just didn't get themselves up like that round here, or see much point in anyone else doing so. Her cheeks became pomegranates set in trampled snow, her eyes were glinting purple caverns, lashed with sooty fibres, her massive ear-rings clipped like locks, and her corsage was elevated, tight and ample. Also, over their mounds of rings, her hands wore white satin gloves, and she carried, held by a bamboo oval round about her encrusted wrist, a bright oriental parasol.

Before departing, she embarked on a tour of the great mansion: not only in those parts of it that were her territory, but even in those forbidden to her which she entered, boldly and deliberately, by means of her pass key. She gazed at each room a moment like a royal favourite contemplating exile (and possibly execution), and stayed longer than at most places in Julius Macnamara's 'study'—which she eyed with proprietory resentment mixed with sadness—and next in his vast and hideous bedroom with its four-poster (imported from Europe by an earlier Macnamara) and its profusion of rather pernickety masculine impedimenta: rows of shoe-trees, rack-like trouser-presses, and a masochistic atheletic contraption, all springs and sliding seats, on which Julius essayed, in vain, to moderate his considerable bulk. At all this—and especially the four-poster with the mysterious bound books on the adjacent bed-table—Mrs Baxter stared with her rouged lips curling but a diluted tear starting in an eye.

Then grabbing her massive hand-bag—it was dyed crocodile, and almost the dimensions of a small travelling valise—Mrs Baxter stepped out into the sun: which glared on her in amazement : . . for surely, at that moment, in the entire district, there was no figure less appropriately equipped to face its rigours than was hers. Mrs Baxter stamped across the great cobbled courtyard to the garages and, after turning back a moment to take in the whole sweep of Macnamara's—the carved wood house, the village of attendant outbuildings, the artesian windmills and the sheep, horses and cattle (and even black swans and tame lyre- and bower-birds) all visible in the home paddocks and on the dams—she wedged herself into her two-seater runabout with the boot rear seat, and backed in jerks towards the automatic gates.

*

By now the tennis was rampaging. On each court were warriors, and round each an attendant throng of vociferous and ironical supporters. Everyone played well, for in this country sport had already become a ritual, and you aspired to championship status from the cradle. The men, with that box-like brawny agility of the Australian male, grasped rackets that looked, in their iron brown fists, like playthings. The girls, if allowing superior strength to the rampant boys, were quite their rivals in force and stamina, and demanded no concessions from the men to their relatively greater frailty. Everyone attacked in the bare sun: and no one gave any quarter, or expected it.

On Maureen and Norman's side of the net, this pair played with concentrated rage: as much against their adversaries, Nancy and Tommy Mulligan, as against each other: for Maureen and Norman were in a high state of peeve. The boy thought, 'I'll show this young tart—I'll win this plurry match even without her.' And Maureen: 'He's not going to treat *me* like a nobody.' So they bashed in silence, occasionally tangling furiously as to who should take a shot, and only speaking when Maureen queried, loud-voiced for all to hear, Norman's declarations that rival shots inside the line, were out.

As for dynamic Nance, she battled with the concentrated will of one who means to dominate her life—and those of others—or else bust. Nothing rattled her, and when she messed up a stroke she made no apology, but swore audibly and gripped her racket all the harder. Tommy, meanwhile, though playing lumpishly without graces, resembled an invisible brick wall: for wherever he stationed himself the ball, it seemed, came his way as if magnetized, and was halted by a power that appeared to extend beyond the normal range of human reach. Only on the backhands was he vulnerable, and each time he missed these Nancy gave him the unforgiving look of she who has already trodden on a good man's hopes.

The game wavered so much between them that, by the time it reached eleven all, complaints were heard from the spectators, and suggestions they call it a draw so that others could take their impatient turn upon the centre court. Three were reluctantly agreeable, but at this point Norman created a slight scandal by announcing vociferously that *he* wasn't going to move until he'd either won or lost. By this gesture, acceptable partly as a proof that he would not be beaten—an attitude the ethos of the district much admired—he had nevertheless broken a more primary social rule which is that, in this country of individualism in the private sector, but rigid conformity in the greater collective, the desires of the one, however legitimate, must yield to the imperative voice of a majority egotism. So when Norman stood his ground, and the other three had retired, he found himself surrounded by four fresh players who began knocking up, ignoring him completely. In a gesture of vengeance, Norman took every ball he could and smashed them back as much at the spectators as at the opposite end of the court. Tolerant laughter greeted this manœuvre for a while, till suddenly the tone altered, and the universal will manifested itself in the shape of two hefty men, far broader and more aluminium-muscled than young Norman, lifting him bodily and depositing him, not gently, on the tired tawny grass verges of the court.

'Well, fuck you all!' said Norman, arising to confront the assembly—who took no notice of him, and concentrated on the game to come.

So Norman threw down his racket and, hands driven deep into the hip pockets of his shorts, he strode off, scratching his bottom furiously, beyond the wire enclosure into the reassuring bush. A 'Coo-ee!' after a moment halted him, and coming panting after, he turned to see Julius Macnamara. 'Yes, yes,' puffed Julius, mopping his crown beneath his panama, 'yes, yes, I saw your demonstration on the courts.'

'Oh—and?' said Norman.

Julius took the boy's reluctant arm and pulled him towards a lop-sided rustic bench combed by acacias. 'We must sit,' he said, 'or in this wicked climate we'll both do ourselves some evil.'

Then Julius offered the annoyed boy a cigar from a serrated leather case which exotic smoke the lad, gratified, accepted. 'I admire your attitude,' Julius said finally, when their cigars were coiling lazily into the surrounding heat. 'Independence of mind and conduct,' he continued, 'is a quality I greatly prize.'

Suspicious, Norman was nevertheless pleased, but cautiously as yet made no reply. The landowner placed a decisive hand on the lad's knee and said to him. 'Now tell me, young man, what are your talents, your intentions, and your prospects?'

Taken aback yet flattered by this unexpected interest Norman answered—the excitement of his recent rage overcoming his natural reserve—'I've finished technical school, did well, work in a sports goods store just now, and I'm studying agriculture nights ready to hike up there to Queensland.'

Julius nodded approvingly, and yet frowned. 'Queensland?' he said. 'But why deprive our fair state of Victoria of your talents?'

'There's more opportunity up there. Especially,' Norman added, darting at Julius a resentful glance, 'if you've not got a bean like I haven't, though you bet I will.'

'True—in a sense true,' rejoined Julius, 'but our state, too, has its opportunities to a lively, active, intelligent young man...' he paused '...who's properly placed.'

There was a silence, Norman quickly scenting some sort of a proposition. 'What does that mean, Mr Macnamara?' he asked guardedly.

The pastoralist sucked thoughtfully at his cigar. 'Listen to me, Culley,' he said slowly. 'As you must know, I am a man of considerable properties. To exploit these, I have a manager but, in the broad direction of affairs, I keep control. Now, I keep control, but I am growing older. Time flies: it exacts its penalties. And I am reaching the stage at which I need... I need a man of trust, of confidence and of ability—a junior prime minister, you might say. Such a man should be young, able, energetic. And perhaps...' Julius paused impressively beneath his aureole of wattles '...and perhaps, Culley, you are such a man.'

'Yes,' Norman answered, 'yes, I dare say I could, at that. But what would there be in it for me, Mr Macnamara? And why are you picking on me out of a clear blue sky?' Norman paused, and gave Macnamara a glance he recognized as being, potentially, as dangerous as his own. 'It doesn't seem to me you're being very precise, you know, and it's facts that interest me more than vague promises.'

Julius smiled and raised his hand for patience, but Norman ignored this angrily, and pressed on (leaving Julius with his mouth open like a fish). 'Yes—what's in it for me in all your plans? If I go up to Queensland, with luck and tough times I can make my way—*my* way, and even become, like you Mr Macnamara, a landowner in my own right. But if I stayed down here, even working for a biggish man like you, I'd be

little better than a high-paid jackeroo. Well yes, I would!'
cried Norman as Julius waved a deprecating paw. 'I'd *manage*
for you, Mr Macnamara, and no doubt get well paid for it, but
if you passed on, your land would go to other Macnamaras.
And I, after toiling for you all those years, I might find I
was out on my arse with just about nothing but a flattering
testimonial.'

Impressed—and a trifle alarmed—by the lad's perspicacity,
Julius nevertheless persisted. 'Let me make a suggestion,
Culley,' he said, 'to you. Come and stay a month or so at my
place! See how you like it—learn from my present manager—
see how you and I get on together: and then, if you're satisfied,
we can bring in lawyers, yours and mine, and talk about some
mutually advantageous contracts.'

Norman, bemused by the thought of lawyers, said, 'Well, I
might consider that.'

'Consider it then!' cried Julius. 'It'll mean leaving your city
job but you would be compensated for that . . . And it'll also
mean, of course, my boy'—Julius paused to prod at the lad with
the butt of his cigar—'that you'll have one hell of a lot to learn,
and that I'll judge you strictly by results just the same as you
will me.'

Norman paused in thought a moment: then remembering his
misadventures of the day, and the desire they gave him to show
Maureen and those rustics who *he* was, and reflecting how he did
need some capital and experience to make a go of it up in the
state of Queensland (still for him the promised land), he suddenly put out his hand (which he held slightly curled as if
crossing his fingers) to clinch the deal. 'We'll have a go at it
then, you and I,' he said.

'Excellent!' cried Julius, pumping the lad's arm. 'And I have
another notion that I think you'll relish!' The pastoralist paused.
'How would it be,' he continued, 'if I offered a job there to
young Nancy, you and she at the same identical time?'

'Nancy? A job?' and Norman gazed into Julius's opaque protruding eyes.

'Why—yes! To look after the house while you learn to undertake the outside work. Not, need I say, as a servant or anything like that, but as an . . . well, an indoor manageress, you might say: the books, the domestic accounts, the residential labours— all the internal economy of the station.'

'You think she'd leave here—this place?' He gazed around. 'This place and all she's got here?'

'Well—I could ask her to, could I not? And what *has* she got here, after all, compared with the sort of position I can offer her?'

Norman considered. It was an agreeable thought in a way, and it would certainly solve one problem for him. But then, he wasn't sure he wanted a girl like Nancy as close around his neck as that. Another thought struck him. 'And what about Mrs Bailey?'

'What about her, Culley?'

'Doesn't she depend on Nance for company and such?'

Julius smiled sagely. 'Oh, no doubt,' he said, 'but I feel sure she'd not stand in Nancy's way . . . or that Nancy would let her, if she liked my proposition. After all, she must realize Nancy won't want to stay in this place forever . . . And besides'—and here Julius's brow clouded slightly—'she'd still have the company of that other girl, Maureen. And insofar as I have judgement,' Julius continued, 'little Miss Maureen is better equipped for the role of perpetual companion. I mean, I don't think she's the marrying kind.'

Norman, as often before, was struck by the lack of realism of the elder generations. 'Oh, you don't?' he said. 'I wonder if you're quite right about that, exactly?'

'In any case,' said Julius emphatically, 'Nancy is my choice: Maureen is not the sort of girl I'd care to have about me.'

'Why: had you thought of having her about you?'

'Certainly not: my choice has long fallen by preference on Nancy, whom I consider more adaptable.'

70

'Well, she's certainly that . . . And suppose,' Norman said frankly, for he was always frank when he was unkind, 'suppose Nancy turns you down?'

Julius smiled complacently. 'As to that, young man, I somehow don't think she will.'

Norman considered. 'You'll not mind me asking,' he said slowly after a while, 'but you haven't any other intentions regarding Nancy, have you?'

Julius mutely raised his brows.

'Yes,' Norman continued, 'it's really just as some sort of a housekeeper you'd want her there?'

'What else?' cried Julius in bland surprise. 'And in any case, dear boy,' he added ingratiatingly, 'with a young lad like you about the place, what chance would *I* have of harbouring other intentions?'

'Yeah. And yet, it might be, Mr Macnamara, that you're asking me so as to make it easier to ask her. And what's more, thinking of getting rid of me once you've got her there.'

Julius smiled and blinked serenely. 'Don't try to probe too closely my intentions!' he exclaimed. 'I've made you an offer and, I think, considering your lack of rural experience, a very fair one. You must just puzzle it all out, and come to the correct conclusion for yourself.'

'Well, I've told you I'm on; we'll just have to see how it all works out.' Norman got up, and looked down sceptically at his possibly future employer. 'But haven't you,' he said, 'already got some sort of a housekeeper down at your place?'

Julius also rose, and confronted with his age and wealth the potency of a younger generation. 'Young man,' he said severely, 'please notice that I have asked you but little about yourself: far less, I am sure, than most men in my position might feel they had the right to, and that indeed they owed it to themselves to do. That is because in all my affairs I work by trust—by instinct. You must please learn to do the same; for if you and I are going

71

to get on, you are not to question me on matters that concern myself exclusively.'

Norman nodded. 'No? Well, fair enough. We'll just have to see what happens, won't we?'

*

Walter Bailey, on his favourite old stable-pony, was riding round the home paddocks checking if sheep might have got entangled in the rabbit wire. It was not strictly necessary for him to do this job, since he had hands who rode out daily watching, among so many other things, for this possibility, but Walter liked to do the men's work sometimes both to keep his hand in and to check. He carried across his saddle a small-bore repeating rifle to take a pot shot at the odd rabbit, if he should see one, so that ambling along across the stony gullies, his appearance was vaguely that of an elderly, improbable bushranger.

As he rode, Walter sang gently to himself: German *lieder* he had learned from old Mrs Bailey, the late beloved matriarch of Cootamundra, and a dedicated amateur musician; and also such portions of Italian and French ballads (heard in earlier days from his wife Helen) of which he could remember the words. These baritone sounds fell peculiarly on the alien Australian air, and Walter found himself raising his voice to make them seem more convincing. For though, in a bare century and a half, white Europeans had secured a solid foothold in the coastal cities of this continent, as soon as you came inland—even to tracts of pastoral cultivation like the district—you were instantly made aware that ancient nature is unwelcoming. Not that these pre-historic hills and whispy clouds of eucalyptus quite reject you . . . it is rather that the weird landscape is utterly indifferent, and waits for you to prove yourself.

Up on the skyline, on his return, Walter saw his wife: for Helen, bemused by heat and tennis squabbles and the load of hospitality, and by a deep yearning in her anxious breast, had wandered out beyond the wattles to be alone a moment and contemplate the open country that often brought her solace. She stood looking beautiful, and vulnerable and alone, and Walter felt again—if only at this distance—the innocence of emotion with which he had first looked at Helen many years ago.

He halted his pony underneath a coolibah, not wishing to disturb this vision, nor give to Helen, should she catch sight of him, the impression he was spying on her; then dismounted, leant his rifle against the tree, and let the pony wander. And in the summer heat, a great exaltation came suddenly to Walter, and the thought that hope, one final time, could be re-kindled. For despite Walter's age, and disillusionment, and self-protective irony, he had never entirely lost the belief, born in us all, that life offers everything provided the heart stays pure: a belief which, once gone entirely, spells the end of all youth and the recognition of decay.

Focusing again, he saw to his astonishment that his wife, like a jelly-fish, had divided into two. He took off and rubbed his spectacles, then looked once more. No, there were not two Helens but Helen and another figure whom he believed, from so far away, to be Norman Culley. Walter swayed a bit, and leant upon the tree, steadying himself against its peeling bark and the cold barrel of his repeating rifle.

A rattling hum behind him caused him to swing round, and shading his eyes once more he saw, jerking noisily across the rutted paddocks, a late arrival whom he soon identified, to his surprise, as Mrs Baxter in her runabout. She was approaching a gate and Walter, had he now climbed back on his pony, could have reached the gate in time to open it for this unexpected visitor. But he felt disinclined to, left the good woman to fumble with the latches as best she could in her high-heeled toeless shoes, and turning again, gazed once more up the hill towards his home. But the figures had disappeared and, rubbing his eyes,

Walter wondered whether the sight of them had not been, in the dancing heat, a pure illusion.

★

'Why, it's you, Mrs Bailey,' Norman said, with that tone of insidious, challenging familiarity he used always to women, yet with a note of deference this time that surprised himself.

'Yes, me, Norman—I'm playing truant from the party for a while. It's wrong of me, I know, but I did suddenly feel so tired and exhausted.'

'Then am I in the road, Helen? You'd like to be alone a bit?'

'Oh no, I didn't quite mean that—you're very welcome, but I think I'll sit down for just a while.'

This Helen did and, as with all her movements, gracefully. Norman squatted in front of her and eyed her with curiosity. 'And you don't play tennis at all yourself, then?' he enquired.

'Not any more—not in this weather, anyway. And besides, Norman, if you're having friends in, there's so much to do you can hardly spend hours out there on the courts.'

'Well, it's a silly sort of game really, I suppose. I mean it's too easy, isn't it, unless you're really a champ. And then, in the doubles, you're always dependent on your partner.'

'What game do you really prefer, then?'

'As a *game* I don't mind tennis, but for *sport* I prefer swimming. You know? You're all on your own in what you do, besides which it's more comfortable, isn't it? I mean it can be competitive if you like, but in races it's just you yourself against the world.'

'You like diving?'

'Love it! High dive for me—I must be a freak, I've got no fear of heights at all.'

'Well, we can't offer you a high dive in our dam . . . but you could have a dip if you really care for one . . .'

74

Norman blushed (to his considerable vexation) and this did not pass unremarked by Helen. 'Oh yes, I've seen your dam,' he said. 'As a matter of fact, Nance took me down there earlier on.'

'To have a swim?'

'Oh no, just to show me around the property when I first came over . . .'

There was a pause. 'You like Nancy?' Helen asked, 'now you've got to know her better?'

'Nance? Why, she's all right.' He looked at her questing eyes. 'Well, I mean she's all right, isn't she? But to tell you the truth, I really prefer the other sheila, though . . .'

'You mean Maureen?'

'Why, yeah. She gets my goat and we had a bit of a row just now, you know. But I like her all the same despite of it. She's a girl who knows her mind and has got her own opinions.'

Helen nodded. 'She's a sweet child,' she said, though without all that much conviction. 'I owe both those girls a lot, really. They've been very helpful to me here in more ways that one . . .'

Norman frowned. 'It's none of my business, Helen,' he said, 'but why exactly do you have those two up here with you?'

'Because I'm often lonely, Norman.'

At the pronouncement of this fell word—absolutely forbidden by the ethos of the district (and indeed of all matey Australia itself)—a tabu was broken, and they were forced to the verge of estrangement or a greater intimacy.

Norman took the plunge. 'Loneliness, Mrs Bailey. You've never had children of your own, then?'

'No.'

'You've not wanted to?'

'Of course . . . Oh yes, I've *wanted* to. But as things have turned out, it hasn't proved to be possible . . .'

Norman looked at her, and wondered both why he felt so sure with her, and equally whether she wasn't just stringing him along for some *purpose*—as all the older generations do! Yet he found himself saying, 'That could . . . is it . . . well, is it that you haven't got on all that well with Mr Bailey?'

Helen stared at him, then quietly began to cry: not a stray tear to be brushed aside and hidden, but a sudden gush. Intensely embarrassed, and much regretting his indiscretion (not because of itself, but because of its consequence of having an hysterical woman on his hands), Norman approached Helen and put his arm round her. She leaned against him sobbing gently, and so they remained for all of several silent minutes. 'I'm so sorry, Norman,' she said at last, 'I've no right to involve you in my troubles, and you must forgive me.'

'Well, Helen, I was a bit nosey, wasn't I,' said Norman.

A gesture so spontaneous as to seem entirely natural—as Norman's clasping Helen and her staying in his arms—now began, to both of them, to seem rather odd. Norman became aware that there was quite a *lot* of Helen . . . that she wasn't just the lively kind of tart or sheila he'd been used to fondling, but a considerable and mysterious presence. And as for Helen, though she shrunk slightly, she felt in this boy a potency and re-assurance she had never fully known before. She looked round at Norman, half shut her eyes, and awaited, as in a trance, her first real kiss of defloration and devotion.

But Norman did not bestow this on her. For despite the respect and admiration for Helen Bailey that was growing in his heart, the vagrant whelp inside him was still strong enough to be instantly suspicious of a condescension by this grand lady, of an attempt to *use* him and impose upon his poverty and youth. Besides, Norman did not like women—even any woman—to make the first advances, as he deemed these inappropriate to his male rights and obligations (a belief which had, hitherto, pro-tected him from insult, while absolutely denying to him any real knowledge of love). So he took away his arm, rather abruptly, and said, 'Yes, well—what about that dip you spoke about?'

Helen sighed deeply—was her great hope always to be unfulfilled?—but instantly, with the schooling of so many years her self-control returned to her like a fetter because she knew that if it never let her dominate a situation, at least it prevented one from wounding her. 'That would be a good idea,' she said, 'if you're sure it's long enough since you had lunch.'

'Well, I don't expect I'll drown: your dam can't be all that deep in this dry weather.'

And before she could reply, he hoisted her rather roughly to her feet and, taking her hand in a dispassionate way (rather as one might lead a pony by a halter), he led her through the steaming matted thickets towards the abrupt expanse, shaded by no single tree, of the gilt water of the dam.

At the last shade he paused. 'What about togs?' he said. 'I didn't bring any.'

'Oh, there's dozens in the shed—of every shape, size and condition. We keep them for visitors, you see, and our own down here as well.' Norman nodded. This lady wasn't going to see him swimming naked if *that*'s what she'd been thinking.

'And yabbies?' he demanded.

Helen, now almost restored to suavity, gave him a silvery laugh. 'I thought you were going to *swim*, Norman,' she said. 'Not just walk along the mud in the shallow end where they can nip you.'

He nodded, and they set off for the shed. Helen stationed herself decorously outside in what scant shade it provided, and Norman entered its darkness, smelling of mud, sweat and evaporated beer bottles. Growing used to the gloom, he stripped and selected the least unalluring of the trunks hanging dried like cardboard upon the rusty walls. Then he emerged and, without a word to Helen, dived in and disappeared.

Mildly alarmed, Helen waited for him to break surface: which he did after two minutes at the far end of the dam, having demonstrated, to his own satisfaction, his prowess at under-water swimming. He heaved himself out, staggered a moment on the muddy bank, then stood in silhouette black-gold against the declining sun. At that distance one could not see Norman's cruelties and weaknesses, which were many, but only that he was a superbly manufactured kid. His dad and mum may have lived in hatred, as he alleged, but at least when they'd come together to make him a grace had descended on their love: for no boy so beautiful could have been created without unity in passion. Norman had the characteristic male Aussie figure carried to the edge of its particular potential of perfection: lithe, tough, mindless and delinquent: fine because of strength and self-contentment more than by any classic grandeur. And his face, as he gazed at the water, was of one, like Odysseus, who would conquer it despite its power; and his ingrown eyes and that taut Aussie curl of the narrow sensual lips, wore an expression of contained unself-critical delight. In this land where to fight nature by being, in the most extreme sense, a part of her, was still a challenge. Norman could confront the elements he was part of with a total confidence. And what mattered, at this moment, the stolen power of his rivals in the district? What, even, mattered a great lady like Helen Bailey?

But how little did this 'great lady' feel herself to be one as she watched the boy! For she felt to be his sister, mother, child even —she felt with this superb single figure on the skyline a unity of heart and body she had never known before! How she longed to cradle him, caress him, to be fondled and sustained by him . . . Yes, though he was so young and she (as she suddenly, bitterly reflected) 'old enough to be his mother'. 'Oh dear God,' she sighed out so softly she could barely hear her own words, 'oh dear God, why does everything come to me so late, and never come?'

*

With the unfailing instinct of the defeated, Mrs Baxter knew whom she should first accost at Cootamundra—a person who shared, despite his posture, her failure, namely Walter. And it was, indeed, a good choice in other ways for one who, as she did, wished to spy out the camp of the complacent enemy. For Walter, like few in the district, had always been polite and affable to Mrs Baxter. Not only because of innate courtesy, but because he genuinely liked her: for someone so different and so palpably vulgar, someone not involved, except in the most superficial way, in the machinations of the district, someone so simple, he felt, despite her 'worldliness', attracted Walter Bailey.

He was polishing his gun when she discovered him. Forced to feign surprise at her arrival, Walter was even more solicitous than usual, and insisted she come in so that he could boil her a cup of refreshing tea (a solace, on whatever occasion, more habitual even than grog or plonk throughout the vast antipodean continent).

Adjusting herself on Walter Bailey's horse-hair couch (a body like Mrs Baxter's always seemed to need a powerful lot of adjustment, with much settling of her huge rear, like a fat cat making itself comfortable), Mrs Baxter plunged into the midst of her theme immediately. No words can describe the frank hideousness of her appalling accent—in which the pronunciation so distorted the words that they seemed almost bereft of their habitual meaning—yet curiously, her speech, for this very reason, carried all the more conviction.

'What I'm really trying to say to you, then, Mr Bailey,' she declared in a nasal soprano that contrasted oddly with her other physical dimensions—'is that Mr Macnamara, in my not so humble opinion, is about to do a bunk so far as I myself personally am concerned.'

'Now please excuse me, Mrs Baxter, what . . . ?'

'Well, not exactly do a bunk, since it's his own home after all and *he*'s not leaving it . . . but what I mean to say is, he wants to get rid of *me* altogether after all these long and faithful years of service.'

'He's dismissing you? But why?'

'Search me, Mr Bailey . . .' she took a great gulp of scalding tea and, apparently fortified by this, cried, 'Oh, after all, why should I kid *you* of all people? No, no, the truth is I know why full well!' Mrs Baxter paused, cup in mid-air, dramatically. 'He wants me to fade away because he wants a young girl down there in my place.'

'You mean . . . as housekeeper?'

'Oh, not exactly *that*, you know.'

'What, then? As his wife?'

'Wife? I don't think *he*'ll ever marry!'

'Why not?'

'Well—has he done yet? And as you know, he's no chicken, is he . . .'

'Then in what capacity, if you're correct . . . does he want this young person there?'

'*That* I must leave to your imagination! After all, Mr Bailey, you may be moral, but you're still a *man*.'

'He wouldn't try to get a young girl there under false pretences . . .'

'Oh, wouldn't he?' Mrs Baxter's violet eyes gazed penetratingly at Walter. 'Now look here, Mr Bailey,' she said vigorously. 'I do believe, by the look on your face, that *you* know more about all this than you're perhaps willing to let on. Well—I'm not one to steal a confidence, or try to. But believe me, whatever proposition he's made, or making, or about to make, to any girl, it isn't honourable.'

'Mrs Baxter!' Walter rose. 'Are you sure it's not because you've had . . . well, I can see some sort of an argument with Mr Macnamara, that you're attributing these motives to him?'

'These whattas?'

'Saying he means to try what perhaps he doesn't?'

'I—tell—you—Mr—Bailey'—she prodded at him gently with her teaspoon—'Julius Macnamara doesn't want wedding bells—not a single one of them.'

'Then he must be mad! How can he think anyone would let him . . . well, let him ever make such a proposition to a young girl if they weren't going to make sure it was an honourable one?'

'But he *has* made a proposition!' Her eyes glinted beneath their accelerating false lashes. 'He *has*, hasn't he? Please come clean now, Mr Bailey—do realize I've come over here, however painful and humiliating it may be, to try to get at the truth!'

Walter put down his cup, looked out of the window towards the courts, looked back, and said, 'Well, yes, I believe he has.'

'You believe so. But don't you know so, Mr Bailey?'

'He said he was going to . . .'

'He said so to you?'

'Yes.'

'And to propose this idea to who? To Nancy, was it? No? Or maybe it was to *Maureen*? It *is* the dark girl, isn't it? Well, isn't it? Oh, please now, Mr Bailey. If we are going to talk about this, either let's be frank, or I'll have to do the best I can with the various parties all by myself. So tell me. It is Maureen, isn't it?'

'Yes: it is.'

'And you let him say this to her?'

'How could I stop him?'

'After he'd told you, you couldn't warn Maureen?'

Walter subsided at his desk. 'Did I have to?' he cried. 'I knew nothing of what you now allege . . . and wasn't it right that *she* should turn him down?'

'You think she did?'

'I don't know . . . I certainly hope so . . .'

'Well—I'll tell you what, Mr Bailey. As I know Maureen, I'll bet you she *did* tell him to go climb a gum tree. And I'll bet you what's more, which is that if she did, he'll have a go next at young Nancy, *and she'll accept him*.'

Mrs Baxter sat back looking triumphant and dejected, if one can imagine such a combination in a human face and body. Walter said, 'But why, Mrs Baxter, do you maintain he's not serious in these strange offers?'

'Look, Mr Bailey! In the first place, you don't talk suddenly of marriage for the first time when you're in your middle fifties. In the second, if my guess is correct, you don't propose to two girls in one single day. And in the third . . . well, I suppose I must be loyal . . .'

'I don't want . . . I don't want to strain your sense of loyalty, Mrs Baxter . . .'

'I do often wonder why I *am* so loyal to him at all. For what has he ever done for me that I should be? Not that I altogether blame the old man, though . . .'

'You mean . . . you still like him?'

'Yes, well, in a way I do . . . I've got used to him, I suppose. Oh yes, I'm fond of him in a way, I dare say. But I don't want to lose my job and position, and I don't want to see him make a young girl miserable, or make a fool of himself, by promising a marriage or anything to her that he can't . . . what's that word?'

'What word?'

'Well, there's a big word for it . . . consummate, isn't it?'

'Consummate? Why shouldn't he? I'm not after all that much younger than he is, yet a man in his middle years can . . .'

'Oh, I don't doubt *you're* all right, Mr Bailey! But as for poor old Julius . . . well, not to put too fine a point upon it—and here I'll have to ask you to excuse my blushes and your own, Mr Bailey—Macnamara, I tell you, is *impotent*!'

'He's what?'

'He can't offer anything at best but a form of marriage—the hollow shell!'

Walter rose abruptly. 'But how on earth do you know that? Do you mean that you and he have . . .'

'Now, now, now, Mr Bailey—don't leap to conclusions, please.

No—cross my heart and hope to die—no, never! Not he and I in any form: not once, not ever, not even when I knew him down in the capital before I came up here.'

'Then how do you *know* what you say is true?'

Mrs Baxter, with an air of absolute triumph, opened her vast hand-bag and took out a bound volume which she slapped vigorously on to Walter's desk. 'Read that some time,' she said. 'It's the old man's diary: his private thoughts.'

'And what does it . . . But Mrs Baxter, you've not purloined this?'

'Of course I've pinched it! I know I oughtn't to, I know it's breaking faith, but I wanted to *know* . . . and I had to bring it here if I wanted to convince you and anyone else interested, didn't I? Well—there it is: just please read it if you doubt my word.'

Walter looked at the book and didn't touch it. 'And what would I find in it?' he asked anxiously.

'What you would find,' said Mrs Baxter, tapping the volume with her ringed gloved hand, 'is that he confesses to himself he's never made it properly with any sheila, and that all he can ever do is—well, you *have* asked for it, Mr Bailey, so I'll have to tell you—all he can do is give himself . . . well, sensations I must leave to your imagination.'

Walter gazed at the book as if it were a serpent. 'You are sure what you say is true—I mean that this volume is authentic?'

'It's all in his writing—he keeps it in secret in his room: and me, as you've guessed, I've had a bit of a read of it.'

Walter, willing to believe the best even of the worst, now assumed the apparel of a cross-examiner. 'But Mrs Baxter, if that were true, why on earth would he want to marry?'

'He doesn't, I keep telling you.'

'Well, to have a young woman living with him?'

'Oh . . . to flatter his vanity—get her in his power—buy her agreement to his whims . . . perhaps he even hopes a handsome young sheila might cure him of his bad habits. Perhaps it's just that he's getting—well, over-eager in his old age: you know, Mr Bailey, the Indian summer those of our age pass through. That's what he wants to do—to try to prove himself, a last attempt before it's quite too late. And at the back of his mind, he may even have the hope that somehow he can get himself an heir.'

Walter broke out from a short silence; 'But my dear Mrs Baxter, really! This is fantastic! And besides, even young girls aren't fools. They'd never agree to live there with him unless he *did* at least agree to marry them . . .'

'No doubt, Mr Bailey. But all I can say is, he'd put *that* off as long as possible—and please don't forget he's got the money as a lure to keep them waiting in suspense. And then, even if he did go through a form of ceremony—legal, I mean—it still wouldn't be what you and I would call a proper *marriage*. I mean, to be frank, in a *double bed*.'

Walter shuddered, looked at her, paused and then said gently, '*I* don't sleep in a double bed, Mrs Baxter, and yet I *do* consider myself to be married . . .'

'Oh you, Mr Bailey—you're different: you're honourable, I mean.'

'I don't know . . . I hope so . . . I wish I were . . .'

Mrs Baxter rose with an effort. 'Well,' she said, defiantly but kindly, 'are you going to *do* anything about all this? Or have I got to? That is, if you believe a single word of what I've said . . .'

He confronted her. 'First tell me again,' he asked, 'can you promise this isn't just a tale you've concocted because Mr Macnamara has given you some kind of notice?'

'No, it's not: you'll have to trust me. I don't deny I'd like to keep the job, and I know I won't do if he gets a girl down there. And I don't at all deny I'm attached to the old fellow, and want to keep him out of harm's way—him as much as anyone else. But the other reason's real enough—it's exactly as I told you, as you can see for yourself if you care to take a glance at that book.'

Walter shook himself, then hurriedly put on a tie and linen jacket. He paused beside the door. 'You'd better stay here,' he said, 'out of the way a bit, and wait for me till I find out what exactly's happening.'

*

Those eliminated in the tennis tournament made their weary way back to the house for tea, more food, and the first of the hard drinks of the later afternoon. And to escape from Tommy Mulligan, Nance had joined a party of young jackeroos (who were telling exclusively male stories) when the exasperated engineer grabbed her and pulled her, despite slaps and shrill protests, into the darkened billiard-room. There he sat her down on the canvas-covered table where she clutched her whisky glass, swinging her legs, and sulking. 'Well,' Tommy said, 'you saw how young Culley behaved himself just now. Well—you saw it, didn't you?'

'Of course I saw,' said Nancy, taking a gulp. 'He was quite right to want to go on playing. I can hold Maureen, but he was getting much too much for you—that boy can *play*!'

'Oh, can he? You're taking *his* side now, are you?'

'Listen, Tommy Mulligan. Haven't I made it clear I'm not under any obligation to you, and I can take whoever's side I want to?'

Tommy clutched her shoulders. 'Is that why you took him down the dam this morning?'

'What if I did?' she cried, shaking free. 'Is that any business of yours?'

'He's a lout, I tell you. A larrikin. And I reckon he's after Maureen now—that shows how much he cares.'

'Well, good luck to him. And as for being a larry, he's a livelier lad than you are, Tommy, let me tell you.'

'Oh, is he, girl!'

'Yes, he *is*. And if I was going to get spliced with anyone, I'd pick him a million times, money or no money, before I ever thought of you.'

A thundering slap resounded throughout the billiard-room. 'You'll regret that, Tommy,' cried Nancy, throwing the rest of her whisky in his face. 'Oh now—come, come, come, come, come!' cried Julius Macnamara, entering and colliding with Tommy Mulligan as he stalked violently out of the room.

'Well!' said Julius. 'A little lovers' tiff, you two? Come, let me replenish your beaker from the decanter here. Me too, I fancy, though the sun's not yet quite over the yardarm. Ah, lovers' quarrels! Youth, youth, youth, my dear—cheerioh!'

'We are *not* lovers, Mr Macnamara. Do please get that straight.'

Julius looked grave. 'I didn't really think so, Nancy. I have always felt sure that a sensible girl like you would look to her main interest if it came to any serious matter.'

'Meaning?'

'Well, meaning not throw herself away on anyone who could not properly support her. Properly, that is, in relation to her youth and considerable beauty.'

Nancy clinked her glass with his. 'I don't mind admitting, Mr Macnamara,' she said evenly, 'that my prime motto in life is to look after number one.'

'Mine too, my dear. To help others, you must first learn to look after yourself. We understand each other, I can see.'

They clinked glasses again.

'Which is more,' continued Julius, after a judicious gulp, 'than can be said for your young friend Maureen.'

'Meaning what *this* time?'

'That she fails to consult her own best interest, and would throw herself away on anybody.'

'How do you know that?'

'Well, I feel it in my bones—my old cunning bones that have lived so long and seen so much.'

Nancy grinned. 'You may be cunning—no one can deny that, Mr Macnamara . . .'

'Oh, come—Julius, if you please . . .'

'Okay, Julius: cunning yes, but you're not really all that old . . .'

'Ah! You'd soon change your tale if I invited you . . . well, if I were to say to you . . .'

'. . . if you said to me, "Nance, why don't you settle down with me?" Is *that* what's hovering on the tip of your bold tongue?'

'Nancy! *You* are a bold young lady!'

'I'm bold all right, and I'm not going to be young forever.' She swayed a bit, and drained a glass now empty. 'Well, Julius,' she said, with sardonic gravity, 'was that little guess of mine correct?'

'Are you serious, my dear? You're not mocking an old fellow?'

'Less of that "old" man, Julius, my boy, and more of the man himself. You're as old as you are, whatever that might be, but you don't strike me as being exactly decrepit.'

'Oh, I should hope not!'

There was a pause, while Julius once more wielded the decanter.

'Well, Julius,' Nancy said with a disillusioned grimace. 'Can I take it I've had a proposition?'

Julius's eyes narrowed, and he retreated from the table just a bit. 'Certainly, my dear! Come with me as soon as you like to be the mistress of Macnamara's station.'

'*Mistress*, Julius?'

'Mistress of the station, and wife of its doubly proud proprietor.'

Nancy slid off the table. 'And you're prepared to repeat those words in front of witnesses?'

'As soon as you wish—immediately!'

Nancy staggered slightly towards him. 'In that case,' she said,

'I suppose you deserve a bit of a kiss from me,' and she gave Julius a wet nibble on the mouth.

'Nancy! I'm overwhelmed,' said Julius, wiping it.

'That's rather the idea,' she said. And withdrawing from him, went on severely, 'But mind you, I want this on the up and up: marriage, settlement, everything I'm entitled to expect.'

'But naturally, my dear. And as an additional attraction,' he continued slyly, 'I can promise you you won't want for young company. For consider, Nancy. Young Norman is coming to the station to be my new jackeroo.'

'That'll make for a lively life . . .' She paused, peering at Macnamara, trying to assess his profundities and weaknesses. Then added sharply, 'And mark this, Julius, I'm not moving in till Mrs Baxter's out and away and long forgotten.'

'That can be arranged,' said Julius, grabbing the girl and gobbling her, each holding a whisky glass behind the other's back.

★

Walter found Maureen, as he had expected, feeding the decrepit cow of whose precarious life she had been the saviour. This cow, on calving, had collapsed with an illness the local vet attributed to some vague word, but hearing it was about to be shot, Maureen had intervened. Not because she was an 'animal lover'—she regarded animals most pragmatically—but because some rural instinct told her that if the beast could only be got on its feet, it might survive. Accordingly, overcoming the mockery of the stockmen, she had persuaded an old-timer on the station to rig up a sort of cradle composed of stout stakes supporting bands of hessian, and into this contraption the laughing stockmen had hoisted the languishing cow where it stood miserably, its hooves barely touching the ground, while Maureen waited for it to confirm her diagnosis by recovering. Thanks to the absolute regularity with which she fed and watered it, twice a day (and to the leafy shelter she had erected to protect it from the sun), the animal showed growing signs of life, and it was now anticipated that it would shortly resume its normal cow-like existence. The only thing that caused Maureen to regret her philanthropic endeavour was that the beast had become nit-infested, so that when, earlier, she had rashly fondled it, she had had (much to everyone's amusement) to be de-loused.

'It will live, Maureen. You've scored a triumph,' said Walter, emerging from nowhere as was usual.

'Oh hullo, Mr Bailey. Yes, the old lady's certainly taken a turn for the better these last few days.'

'And you were proved right when we all were wrong,' said Walter, '—good for you.'

Surprised by this most unusual bestowal of praise, Maureen said nothing, but continued to resist the cow's attempts to push the water-bucket out of her hands with its livelier sucking head.

He stood watching her. My goodness! thought Walter, you can certainly tell these days what a girl *looks* like—not as in the more swaddled days when he'd met Helen. A shirt, shorts and white shoes (and doubtless the merest of underclothes) revealed all any man could want to know of Maureen's figure . . . which, to himself, Walter had always described as welcoming: ample but lithe, all of an easy piece, very female but not too 'feminine' . . . and above all, practical: a useful, helpful and seductive body was what Maureen possessed. Eve must have been like this, he thought—or was she? (Was Eve the temptress, or the liberator?) And as for her face, well, no one could call it beautiful, or even pretty, but it was undeniably attractive—frank and serious and ever so slightly mocking in a non-judging kind of way. Thinking of all Mrs Baxter had said, and of any thought of Maureen's marrying anyone, Walter suddenly realized how much he might miss the child he had always taken so completely for granted round about the station.

'Yes—right when we were all wrong: one up to you, Maureen.'

'Thanks, Mr Bailey.' She put down the bucket and rubbed the cow's nose (but not its hair).

'But Maureen,' Walter continued, looking grave, 'you must try to be right too for yourself as well as to a four-legged creature that you've saved for me.'

Sensing a lecture, Maureen grew guarded yet attentive.

'You know, Maureen,' Walter continued, lighting one of his unexpected cigarettes, 'just because I've done so little for you, I've also tried not to interfere with you . . .'

'Oh, but Mr Bailey, you've been ever so . . .'

'No, no, you've earned your keep here, as you know, and owe me nothing. But all the same, I was trying to say I do feel, as the head of the household here, in some ways responsible for you: for your welfare.'

'Oh yes, Mr Bailey?' she said rather coldly. 'Thank you.'

'Now at this point, Maureen,' Walter said, casting his eyes about and tapping an ash that didn't yet exist, 'you are fully entitled to tell me to mind my own business.'

'About what?'

'I may go on, then?'

She laughed. 'Well, of course, Mr Bailey—until I know what it is! It's a girl's privilege to be inquisitive, but to prevent anyone else being it to her, isn't it?'

Walter smiled too, then grew solemn. 'Look, Maureen: don't answer at all if you don't feel inclined to: but this morning, Mr Macnamara revealed to me that he thought of asking you something which . . . well, I don't know if he has . . .'

Maureen frowned. 'Oh, so he spoke to you about it first. I wish he hadn't . . .'

'You minded my hearing about . . . his intentions?'

'Not that, exactly . . . but the whole thing—everything he said to me—was so ridiculous, that I'd rather no one knew except him and me.'

'And—and what did you say to him?'

'What do you imagine?' Maureen laughed again, a bit tightly. 'I just told him not to be so silly—which he really was.'

'You did, did you, Maureen?'

'Of course I did. And just to think! My very first proposal of marriage, and it turned out a sort of comedy! It's not a very romantic start in life, is it?'

'I'm so glad you take it that way—I mean don't take it all too seriously. And you don't think . . . you don't think, Maureen, that since he spoke to me first, I should have warned you he was going to do so to you too?'

'No, Mr Bailey. It wasn't really your concern, if you'll excuse my saying so, and it wasn't at all hard for me to say no . . .'

'That's a relief to me, Maureen: that, and the fact that you . . . told him he was silly . . . That's an even greater relief to me . . .'

'Why, Mr Bailey! You didn't ever think I'd take him seriously?'

'One never knows, Maureen. Girls are mysterious creatures, and after all, I really don't know you all that well . . .'

'Well enough to know I've got a bit of common-sense . . . *plus*, I do hope, a certain amount of self-respect,' said Maureen severely—surprising herself at rebuking a man she had hitherto held somewhat in awe, and realizing yet again (as she had come to do more and more) that those older than herself were not always so 'wise' as they had so often implied to her they were.

'And I respect you, too, Maureen,' said Walter rather hastily, 'for your good sense and decent pride. All the same,' he continued, 'if I might offer just one word of advice, please don't do anything further to aggravate Mr Macnamara . . .'

'But how have I aggravated him? Wasn't it really the other way around? I mean, didn't he take a liberty with me?'

Walter, feeling his advantage in years rapidly shrinking, and her young wisdom growing all the time, added quickly, 'No— all I meant was, Macnamara has his vindictive side, and as he possibly feels a bit humiliated—well, you can understand that, even though it *was* his fault—please, if you will, don't give him . . . well, don't rub his face in the clay, or he might possibly try to harm you.'

'Oh, Mr Bailey!' She gave him a frank smile. 'Do you know what I want to do with dear old Mr Julius Macnamara? Just keep out of his way till he's calmed down and turned his attention to his prize sheep and cattle where it ought to belong!'

'Good!' Walter cried. 'You're a *good* girl, Maureen,' he added quietly, surprising her by the insistence of his look (till she almost thought—Well, *this* old man's not going to make a pass at me too, is he?). 'Good, dear. And all I can say is, I do hope you'll soon find the right man, worthy of you, and that you'll be happy as you deserve . . . though of course, when that day comes, I shall be most sad to lose you.'

'Thanks: thanks a lot, Mr Bailey. Well,' she added, half comically, as she picked up the bucket (as if *she* was bringing the interview to a close), 'I reckon when the right man comes, *I*'ll know who he is all right.'

'And he hasn't yet?' Walter asked kindly.

She started a little and shot him a swift glance. 'I'm not so sure,' she said softly, 'but when he *does*, as I say, I'll *know* it.'

Walter took the bucket from her, with the 'old-world' polite-ness Maureen always found, frankly, on the rare occasions when she met him, a bit embarrassing. For Aussie girls (often quite rightly) imagine such gestures are a masculine device for under-mining their cherished independence. He further surprised her by taking her arm and saying gravely, 'I do hope you'll be happy, Maureen—for it's something that has always eluded me . . .'

A bit exasperated by this confidence (adults *shouldn't* reveal their feelings: aren't they supposed to be stronger or, at any rate, always claiming that they are? They can't have it *both* ways), Maureen turned to him and said, 'And why has it eluded you, Mr Bailey?'

92

Any revelation that might have resulted from an exchange of their strengths and weaknesses was interrupted by the sight of a frieze of stockmen, looking, as Australians astonishingly do, so like those Athenian sculptures in which the men and their horses are no longer separate entities, but that single creature of antiquity, the *horseman*. There were waves and cracks to Maureen (mostly relating to the recuperating cow), and egalitarian cries of 'Evening, Mr Bailey' to the proprietor. And as they passed lazily to the sheds—the groups of riders forming and re-forming constantly, with figures turning on their horses to call back to others, so that the frieze, in the glowing fall of the sun, became momentarily perfect—Walter was anxious to resume the exchange, but the moment had passed, for Maureen said briskly:

'Well, thanks for taking the bucket, Mr Bailey, and I can certainly tell you this. I don't want to cause anyone trouble—anyone—but if any man takes undue liberties with me, I've got all my brothers down there in the south who will march straight up to the district—or to anywhere else in the country—and stoush whatever man is crook in any serious way to their young sister.'

Walter opened his mouth to answer—and to assure her that here at Cootamundra, at any rate, he would protect her in such an event if only he knew it had happened, or was about to (which of course, he would never know)—when his speech was cut short as he turned to the sight, on the edge of the track leading up to the house, of his lost wife Helen.

'Well, too-a-roo and thanks, Mr Bailey,' said Maureen briskly, determined to avoid any other 'scenes': and she left him moving quickly away as she sent a 'Coo-ee!' after his wife, who had as swiftly disappeared again up the track from whence she had come.

*

Helen waylaid Maureen on the path, and the girl perceived at once that the older woman was 'distraught': a word Helen herself used to describe these occasions—increasingly rare, fortunately—when she appeared suddenly wild-eyed, and even (unlike her) a bit unkempt, and excused herself to the girls by using this unpleasant word: whereupon she would retire, if possible, to her bedroom and, like Walter (at any rate for a while), would not be seen for a day or even two. But now with the party, Mrs Bailey could not retire; and Maureen, who had just handled one adult, realized, with reluctance and annoyance, she might have to do her best to calm another.

'Why, Mrs Bailey!' she said, taking the older woman's arm. 'Aren't you a bit fagged out? What about a lie-down before the supper?'

'What was my husband saying to you, Maureen?' cried Helen, abandoning her habitual discretion and aplomb.

'He was on about that silly old cow of mine, and passing the time of day in a general sort of way.'

'He didn't speak to you about . . . Macnamara . . . marriage . . . a suggestion he says he made to you?'

Gorblimey! thought Maureen: does every bloody body at Cootamundra know the old goat tried to make a fool out of me? Or is she just guessing? 'No, no, Mrs Bailey,' she said, 'he wasn't on about anything like that . . .'

'But there has been converse between you and Macnamara of that nature?'

'Oh, enough said about all that, for Pete's sake!' cried Maureen briskly.

'About marriage?'

'Now, now, now, Mrs Bailey. Even if there was, isn't it honestly my sort of business, and perhaps his, but at any rate nobody else's? Please don't think me rude, now, will you, but as nothing's going to come of it, I do think I'm entitled to keep my little secrets to myself.'

94

Abashed, Helen Bailey recovered something of her habitual exterior calm. 'Oh, excuse me, Maureen. It has been so *hot*, hasn't it—I mean exceptionally so, and the guests are becoming so noisy and so quarrelsome, and I do believe, for the first time I can remember, I almost wish we didn't have all these perpetual Saturdays at Cootamundra.'

What *you* need, thought Maureen, is a smack on the arse, a lie down, and perhaps a couple of pink gins. 'You're just tired a bit,' she said consolingly. 'What about a shower, a short nap, and then a swift grog before we serve them supper?'

'You're wise, dear . . .' Helen took her hand, which Maureen rather reluctantly gave her, and they started walking up the track. 'Yes, I've been upset . . . so many feelings . . . so many people . . . so many distractions on this long hot day . . .'

Oh, the older generation, Maureen thought once again! Will *I* ever be as dopey as they are when I get to be their age? No self-control—well, that doesn't matter so much (who has it, anyway?)—but not even any sense of what they want and what they don't. Honestly, I'm beginning to think 'experience' simply means you get softer and sillier every time the same thing happens to you all over again!

The sound of voices from the courts in the final games of the tournament halted Helen once more in her tracks. 'Will that competition *never* be over?' Helen cried. 'Can't they call it a draw and come in for rest and some refreshment?'

'Oh, Mrs Bailey! A tournament's a tournament up here . . . You remember the time they went on till midnight with the cars parked all round the court with their headlights shining?'

From the courts, as they waited, came the cries of the ad hoc umpire yelling, 'Fifteen-love, Thirty-love, Forty-love—Game!'

'Why is it called "love"?' said Mrs Bailey suddenly.

'Search me: they're not exactly love matches we play up here, are they? They're more like battles between Amazons and cave-men.'

'Games five-love,' cried the umpire, 'sets two-love: this looks like the clincher, kiddos—why on earth did you come up against our star players in your finals?'

'But why does "love" mean "nothing"?' repeated Mrs Bailey.

Growing impatient, and dying for a dip (and to wash the cow smells off her), Maureen said, 'Coming on up to the house?'

Helen now faced her. 'Maureen,' she said: 'Do you love anyone here today?'

'Do I *whatta*, Mrs Bailey?'

'Love anyone here? Any of the guests or visitors?'

'Well, what a question! Certainly not old Julius, if that's what you're hinting . . .'

'But any others? J G, Tommy . . . Norman?'

Well, well, well, thought Maureen. Can you bloody-well-beat-it!

'Mrs Bailey,' she said firmly and almost unpleasantly. 'My heart is free, I'm not signed up with anyone, please believe me.'

'Then may I tell you something?'

'Well, now look, Mrs Bailey, don't you think we'd better . . .'

'Maureen! I am in love with this boy Norman!'

'Oh!'

'Oh, yes, I know what you'll say . . . it's unsuitable . . . I'm too old . . . he's too young . . . he doesn't care for me anyway . . . but the feeling is so strong, so powerful, so overmastering, that I just had to confide in someone and tell *you*.'

Well, I wish you bloody well hadn't, Maureen thought. 'Oh, come off it, Mrs Bailey,' she said briskly. 'It's what they call summer fever, tennis passion—you know . . . we all feel like that at times about someone on a hot Saturday, don't we?'

'You do too?'

'Tell you a secret, Mrs B: I was crazy about one of the shearers for a whole week! Such a handsome boy—so cheeky, a Queenslander he was, who'd travelled over the whole country, shearing!'

'But Maureen: what do you *think* of Norman?'

Tearing herself away irritably, Maureen said abruptly: 'That he's a skite, a larry, a blodger and a drongo all rolled into one. That's my frank opinion—so do be sensible, Mrs Bailey. He's not worth the turds anyone walks on . . .'

'Maureen!'

'Well, he isn't. And that's all I've got to say and really, Mrs Bailey, I must get up to the house and soap my legs and change into a dress and have a spot of plonk or I'll go crazy. Coming?'

But as Helen stood gazing at her, Maureen cried briskly, 'Too-a-rooster, then!' and darted off up the track. Helen, left solo, holding her hand up to her neck, gazed after her, then turned as she heard voices calling, amid yells of laughter, 'Love game, six love, game and set!'

'Love all! Love all! Love all!' cried Helen Bailey.

★

Boozers from the house, carrying filled glasses and even bottles, had come back to the courts to watch the final set of the tournament: to jeer and cheer from the comfort of showers, changed clothes, and half a dozen drinks inside their bellies, at the still sweating and exhausted players as they lammed away into the rising gloom of the vanishing sun. The big joke of the afternoon was that, by a freak of the games, the district doubles champions (who had mysteriously drawn each other—above-board? couldn't be; surely J G Eaton, who'd organized it, being half blind, had been fooled!) were defeating ingloriously a hopeless young pair who'd nevertheless precariously survived until this final game. The spectators rooted for the rabbits, but secretly hoped the champions would make mince-meat of them—which they did.

Norman, clutching a scotch chased with lager beer, spotted

Maureen after the game finally collapsed, and the party all trooped back vociferously to the house. He ran up and offered her a swig which she was too exhausted to refuse and then, looking virtuous, said, 'Hadn't someone ought to let down all the nets? They've forgotten as usual, needless to say.'

'You do it, then: I want my dip.'

'Oh, come on, Maureen—lend the man a helping hand.'

He grabbed hers, and they went back to the lonely courts. Though Maureen was fascinated by Norman (and just as peeved with him because of his earlier behaviour), the recent exchange with Helen made her reluctant to be with him just for the moment: not that she wouldn't take on Helen—or *any*body—in a battle for a man she herself was keen on, but she felt a scruple about hurting the older woman (still in the vicinity!) despite her now appearing as a rival (and one Maureen didn't by any means underestimate: you could see how often these young boys were impressed by elder women, and their vanity flattered by a conquest!). So she hurried him up from net to net, and resisted his peace-making jests and conceited witticisms.

All the same, he was rather sweet, the dirty young dog: and looking ever so nice in pale slacks, a clean white shirt and his championship blazer. And there was no denying he was strong and not a coward, and a boy with personality who would certainly get *some*where some day, even if it was the inside of Pentridge prison. But too cocky, too rough, too bloody pleased with his bloody self . . . Maureen liked boys who liked themselves, but she preferred them to have thoughts left over for somebody else, especially for her . . .

'I dare say,' she said, 'if you hadn't played with me *you* might have won the tournament yourself today.'

'Oh, if they'd only let us go on, we'd have made it all right . . . what's the prize, anyway?'

'It's a tame bandicoot this week. They're keen on joke

prizes up here, though personally I'd prefer some cash or anything else valuable.'

'Me too. What can you do with a bandicoot, tame or otherwise? It's just as well we lost.'

With a sudden generous thought (and a small slice of venom towards Helen also?) Maureen said, 'Well, I'll give you a consolation prize: here, catch!' and she threw to Norman Helen's opal in its little wad of cotton-wool.

He examined it in the fading light and said, 'Oh, pearla— it's a beaut. And look at it winking. Just like your eyes, Maureen.'

'That'll be enough of that, son. One more net to lower.'

He put his arm round her, but cautiously and gently this time. 'Oh, you do like me, Maureen, don't you?' he said appealingly, with an urchin grin he had often found effective.

'I'll like you when you're likeable,' said Maureen, disengaging his arm.

She lowered the last net, and Norman watched: and the sun chose this moment to wink over the edge of the far horizon by the radio masts. 'Back across there tonight, and back to the old city tomorrow evening,' Norman sighed. 'More work for the undertaker, Maureen: there's no rest for the wicked and the wage-slaves of this world.'

'Come on then—I can hear they've put on the gramophone, and there'll soon be dancing.'

'Can you do the Black Bottom? Take a look at this!' And Norman executed around the court a tracery of grotesque and hideous steps.

'Fox-trot and waltz is okay for me,' said Maureen. 'Come on up.'

'Waltz? Just watch my smoke!' Norman glided in her direction, seized her and twirled her round the court to the far distant notes of *What'll I Do?*

'Rubber on asphalt doesn't make much of a dancing floor,' said Maureen, trying to extricate herself.

'Then let's sit this one out,' said Norman softly, pulling her towards the verge and suddenly throwing her with all his strength down on the ground.

But Maureen was not a country girl (with six strong wrestling brothers) for nothing. After a heave or two and several frustrated smacks, she kneed Norman vigorously in his genitals.

'Bitch! Whore! Tart out of Little Lon!' cried Norman, massaging himself violently, and trying to fall on her again. But Maureen had scrambled up and fled, and as Norman chased after her, a posse of guests from the big house fell on him and carried him struggling off towards the ancient, nearly empty well.

★

For the guests, in Norman's absence, had all agreed that a fitting punishment for his earlier ill-conduct would be to rope him up and lower him into the old well on the pretext of seeing if there was any water left in it. This could, of course, have as easily been ascertained by lowering a plumb-line (or even throwing a stone down and listening), and in any case the water was infected and undrinkable; but this personal inspection was deemed necessary by the committee of honour of young (and intoxicated) jackeroos who had now seized on Norman.

The whole scene was proof of the *boyishness* that survives in anglo-saxon adults, and expecially among Australian males: that sudden reversal of six-footers in their middle twenties to the practices and ethos of the lower forms at school. And what was not perhaps surprising was that the Aussie boy-girls joined in the fun as well—if only as encouraging spectators—so that when Norman was forcibly stripped, he was allowed to keep on his underpants for minimal decorum. Nor did the older men, although they hardly approved (after all, such jests are notoriously dangerous), have the spirit to interfere, so strongly did the boy-man instinct grip them also. So the lid of the rotting wood cover to the well was lifted, a sheep-shank knotted across Norman's chest and under his arms, and amid cheers from the assembly he was lowered slowly into the stinking gloom.

As soon as he reached the water, Norman found he was out of his depth so, diving quickly into the slime, he got out of the knot, and surfaced on the far side of the wide well . . . surfaced, in fact, beside the floating, rotting, corpse of a long lost cat. Here he kept silent, ignoring the festive mocking calls that descended, echoing, down the slippery dark-green walls of the well, from the dim square of light above, through which the faces of his executioners were craning. A torch was soon flashed, and when they saw him nowhere, Norman, to his satisfaction, heard a note of anxiety in their chatter, and soon—as he had anticipated—the ringleader of the squad, a hefty jackeroo from beyond the township, was lowered in his turn as a one-man rescue party. As this boy carried the torch, Norman submerged again when he came nearer, swam underneath the glutinous water (trailing the cat), reached up, and with all his strength tugged the boy down by the legs and held him as long as he could underneath, at the same time contriving to rip off the invader's underclothes. Surfacing, he attached the cat to the rope and gave a tug: the vile corpse ascending dangling—to be greeted with alarm as with somewhat frenetic laughter. Meanwhile Norman sought out his tormentor and hit him as hard as he could from behind with a floating plank (with nails in it) which he had located. The boy passed out, and Norman sustained him, treading water, and crying up to the surface, 'Your big pal's fainted—you'd better come down and get him before I let him sink.'

By now there were wild shrieks from the girls, and angry shouts from the older men (who should, of course, have taken action earlier), and more ropes and volunteers were lowered for the rescue of Norman and the wounded boy. No one asked, when they all surfaced, how the supine jackeroo came to be covered in blood, but everyone guessed, and gazed at Norman oddly: this was *not* how to take a good old Aussie joke. But Norman confronted them standing alone and said to them all (to the older men also), 'Anyone else like to come down with me? Any offers? Or I'll take two of you down there if any single one of you's scared . . .'

'That's enough now,' said Tommy Mulligan, hustling forward from the phalanx of older men who were succouring the youth with the cracked skull.

'You,' said Norman to Tommy slowly, 'can just piss up your skinny wet leg.'

Mulligan hit Norman hard and knocked him over, whispering, 'That's for Nance!', and before Norman could retaliate, J G Eaton (who turned out to be unexpectedly wiry) pinioned him from behind and cried, 'Now really, Norman! You're not out with the Fitzroy push just at the moment!' Norman said, 'Oh well, I suppose you've all had your bit of fun . . . But if there's any more of it'—and he gazed balefully at them all— 'I *am* warning you that it won't just be a smack over the head, it will be a *lethal wound*.' Then he stalked up to the house to wash (and change back into his tennis shorts again), leaving the guests angry and hesitant and muttering.

At the house, all was splendid confusion. The girls—guests as well as hosts—were preparing supper, the men were getting drunk, and having the time of their lives moving the furniture and lifting the carpet in the great saloon for the impending dancing. Someone spilled flour on the floor—to make it easier on the feet; and when the gramophone played a Hawaiian number (recorded in New York?), Julius Macnamara (who had actually been out there) sent everyone into fits by putting on a giant lamp-shade as a grass skirt, and performing an extremely vulgar hula-hula dance. Not to be outdone, Nancy appeared wrapped in a blue bath towel in the form of a sarong, and cavorted with her possibly future spouse. Then the girls appeared from the kitchens, and that form of entertainment peculiar to Cootamundra (and indeed to the surrounding district) —the perpetual supper, dance, and alcoholic carnival, all taking place together—swung into agitated, noisy, thoroughly agreeable, not very beautiful action.

Some surprise was caused when Mrs Baxter, erupting from no one knew where (in fact, she had escaped from the purdah to which Walter had consigned her), appeared at the big bar on the side veranda. Everyone was courteous, and wondered whether Julius had sent for her, or whether she had possibly arrived bearing some fell tidings. The men—especially the older men— plied her with liquor (for Mrs Baxter was known to be a solid toper, who could hold her own with any man . . . and in her cups, a superb raconteuse of 'risqué' stories of her earlier life), and gathered round her admiringly. But she kept asking for Maureen, and Nancy, though no one led her to them since Nancy was thought to be too drunk (and was known to be behaving in the saloon somewhat outrageously with Julius), and with their rather old-fashioned—Victorian, almost—attitude to the older woman (so much contrasting with their camaraderie towards the young), the elder men felt it would be indecorous— however drunk they all were themselves—for Mrs Baxter to see Nancy in this condition. As for Maureen, though a superficial search was made, she was nowhere to be found.

As a matter of fact, Maureen was out in a home paddock gazing at the Southern Cross. She adored this group of stars which is indeed the most miraculous of those of both hemispheres, since its bright precision, and its so well-determined shape, have the quality of a legend, and no stars seem to indicate a way, a path, a message, more clearly and insistently (hypnotically, almost, although inscrutably) than does this lovely, slightly irregular crucifix of gleaming light. She thought of Norman, and what a damn *pity* it was he was so impossible, so hopeless, treating her like that—and himself too, come to think of it—for she now realized that she loved him. And she thought of poor old Helen, and wondered what on earth would become of her if Norman, as she expected (and hoped as well), laughed at her elderly illusions, and caused her a new pain to add to the old one that she shared with Walter.

As for Helen, she was doing something she had not done for more than twenty years: which was kneeling by her bed, hands clasped like an infant and, with slightly hysterical conviction, praying. Her prayer was, 'Oh give me Norman's love and if that be denied me, reconcile me with my husband Walter before I am too old.'

Walter himself had gone out again with his gun and was trying to shoot the kookaburra that mocked him daily, outside the annexe, with its raucous, sardonic laughter. He knew where it nested, and had hopes of taking its insulting life in the innocent danger of the night.

*

The eventual encounter between Nancy and Mrs Baxter occurred near a place where unexpected meetings often do—the lavatory. Nancy was trying to get in and rattling the door, when Mrs Baxter emerged (as if from the portals of Government House) and caught Nancy unawares. But she rallied and cried, 'Hullo, old duck! Hold this glass for me, will you, while I powder my Clara Bow nose, or so they tell me?'—then disappeared inside for rather a long while.

Mrs Baxter waited patiently on a settee in the corridor, firm on her enormous bottom, and clutching her hand-bag like a shield. Nancy, on emerging, had evidently thought up words of contumely and defiance in that great place for imaginary dialogue, and said to the older woman, swaying slightly, 'Well, as I expect you know, old girl, you'll be getting the order of the boot.'

'Come and sit down, Nancy.'

'No—I want a drink.'

'Here's your drink . . . come and sit down, because I've things you ought to hear.'

With what she imagined to be a cynical vamp smile, Nancy sat astride one of the thick arms of the settee. 'I'm all ears, old lady,' she remarked, tossing back a noggin.

'I believe,' said Mrs Baxter, 'that Macnamara's made a certain suggestion to you.'

'You make it sound indecent, but yes—old Julius has.'

'And you're accepting?'

'You bet: when he says the word in front of witnesses and lawyers.'

'And you think he will?'

'Well, dearie, either he does or he doesn't. If he does—bontoshter. If he doesn't—well, no little Nancy for Mr Julius Macnamara. I'm easy either way, old Mrs Baxter.'

'So you don't care for him, then.'

Nancy tried to look ruminative, though succeeding chiefly in looking drunker. 'Yes and no. My dream man, of course, is Rudolf Valentino . . . or I'd settle for Richard Barthelmess at a pinch. But failing them, I'm prepared to say yes to any man who'll give me a decent kind of *independent* life.'

'And you'd get that with Macnamara?'

'I believe so: yes, I believe so, old lady—that I do.'

Mrs Baxter raised and lowered her bag on her huge knees. 'And my dear, nothing disgusts you about this kind of an arrangement?'

'Not if it's marriage—no.'

'The difference of your ages? Julius's character?'

'Look, Mrs Baxter—I'm not altogether a loon. I'm *not* marrying Julius Macnamara for love, if that's what you mean.'

'I see. But marriage means certain duties—that thought doesn't disgust you?'

'No. I'll be frank with you, Mrs B. Sex, to me, is just a sensation—nice or not so nice, according. And to be franker still—and you can repeat me if you like, but it won't do you much good because *he* isn't a fool either—I don't suppose my future husband will be the only man in my existence.'

'No, I can see that. But so far as he is, *that* won't disgust you?'

Nancy contemplated her empty glass. 'Yes, I suppose it will, a bit. But I consider the game is well worth the candle.'

'And it wouldn't disgust you . . .' Mrs Baxter continued slowly, '. . . to think your future husband has certain physical peculiarities?'

'Oh, has he? Such as what? And how do *you* know, anyway? Just as well you're leaving, dearie, isn't it.'

Mrs Baxter rose. 'Nancy,' she said, 'I think you ought to know Mr Macnamara isn't enabled.'

'Isn't whatta?'

'He's not a full man: he cannot do what every husband ought to.'

Nancy stared up at her, then burst into cackling laughter. 'The old boy isn't *enabled*? Good! Fine! So much the better—that'll leave me all the more time for the others.'

'You'd share your life with a man like that?'

'Wouldn't you?'

'Not as his wife . . .'

'Oh, come off it!'

'And I'm an older woman, anyway, not a girl . . .'

Nancy rose too. 'Look, lovely,' she said earnestly. 'I'm a poor kid and I want *money*: I want house, cars, clothes, travel, something in my own name in the bank—the lot. It may not be nice, but please admit I'm frank about it. If Julius wants some slap and tickle, okay, I'll pull a sheet over my head and grin and bear it. If he doesn't, or can't, okay too, so long as he sees me right financially.'

'Nancy, I think you are a slut.'

'And what are you?'

'An older woman is never a slut—she's just a misfortune.'

Nancy dropped her glass on the floor and stood arms akimbo. 'Look, I don't care what I *am*, I do care what I want to *get*. It's my life, after all. If Julius wants bed, or none, or excitements watching me and Norman . . . or me with one of the shearers, I don't care . . . well, if I fancy the lad, that's quite okay with me.'

'You *are* disgusting, dear. I'm sorry for you.'

'And I am for you. I'm honest: what *you* really want is not to protect me in the slightest, but stay on in a soft job at Macnamara's—which, if *I* have anything to do with it, you're bloody well not going to.'

'No, Nancy. If I lose, I lose. But I like Julius enough to try to make sure *he* doesn't make a fool of himself, and suffer.'

'Any man of his age who wants to marry a girl of mine is doing something foolish. You know that, and I do, and I expect he does too, and doesn't care.'

'You don't know him: any more than he really knows himself.'

This dialogue was interrupted by yet another visitor to the same indispensable little room—this time Maureen. And for reasons inexplicable even to Nancy herself (perhaps the most hateful feeling of all, that here was a more *wonderful* person!), Nancy cried out, 'Here comes the wonder girl of Cootamundra. Has Norman kept his promise to me yet about you?'

'What does that mean, Nancy?'

Nancy stared, blinked, swayed, then, tottering slightly, made off again towards the corridor. At the end of the passage she looked back, smiled to herself, and said, 'I wouldn't even put it past this serious young lady to end up with Walter in the annexe. Then we'd *both* have our demon lovers.'

Her exit left Maureen and Mrs Baxter, for different reasons, somewhat confounded. Maureen's chief regret was that she had lost, in that moment, what she had had hitherto in Nancy— a friend. Mrs Baxter's regret—a deeper one—was that somehow her own life had *never* turned out as she had hoped. (She still felt so young!).

'Hey—you're crying, Mrs Baxter. That won't do.'

'Just a touch of the hysterics, dear. Take no notice.'

'Would you like a drink or something?'

Mrs Baxter, drying her eyes, looked suddenly prim. 'I mustn't detain you, my dear,' she said, 'from doing what I know you must have come here to do'—and she waved politely towards the lavatory door.

'Okay,' said Maureen smiling. 'I'll get you a glass when I emerge.'

She soon did, and found Mrs Baxter admiring a painting of the explorer Charles Sturt, who had passed this way nearly a hundred years before. They looked at each other and sat down again. 'And what's the matter with Nance?' said Maureen.

'She's been telling me some home truths: my silly old fault, I suppose, for confiding in her.'

'Was it . . . about Mr Macnamara?'

'Oh yes, it *was*. And I dare say *you*'ve had a little session with him earlier on, too, haven't you? And if I know you, Maureen, you told him not to be so bloody silly as he's going to be with Nancy.'

'What! Has he asked *her* too, now?'

'He has . . .'

'Well, he *is* a bit desperate, isn't he? And she's accepted?'

'What do you suppose?'

'That she's accepted: poor old Nance!'

'Yes,—poor old Nancy . . . or is she? You know, it's a sad reflection, but sometimes I believe that we do all get what we want in the end . . .'

'Oh, you believe that?'

'Yes, I do . . . almost. Perhaps what *I*'ve really wanted is a half-life like I've had . . . though I did have good times with dear old Baxter when we were younger . . .'

Mrs Baxter sniffed again; then said, 'And you, Maureen? What do *you* want?'

'Me? Me, Mrs Baxter, I want love.'

Mrs Baxter took her hand. 'Then I expect you'll find it, Maureen, if my theory's right. Though believe me, it's the hardest thing in the world to get, the most painful to endure, and the easiest of all to lose.'

★

At a dance, or 'hop', up in the district, the essential quality of the performers is a driving physical energy, absolutely indefatigable. Good dancing is of course appreciated: that is to say, to be too 'fancy' is to be dubbed a skite, but genuine, apparently effortless prowess is admired, for Australians respect all physical accomplishments . . . at any rate, those athletic or even vaguely so. On the other hand, to dance badly, in a boy or girl, is excused provided either shows this elemental gusto. Once again, Australians, though they mostly like to do as little as possible of anything (except just that) do demand, when something *is* undertaken, that it be undertaken thoroughly.

J G operated the gramophone—and, because of his myopia, often announced a waltz but put on a quick-step; and, in most cases, jabbed the needle down at peculiar moments in the tune. Since the records, anyway, lasted only a few minutes, most couples danced on between the pauses for changing them over, and altered their steps when the new records blared on. There was quite a lot of necking, but of a very public kind, for this was thought seemly—nay, called for if the sheila was attractive—whereas real eroticism would have been considered quite amiss (Australians are a hot-blooded, not a sensual people). There was also a most prodigious lot of drinking, but in the hot night, and with the violent exercise, most of the performers managed to sweat their intoxication out.

At a general pause for supper, Julius was consuming tinned lobster and talking radio with Tommy Mulligan and J G. 'I'm glad I sold your people that land up on the plateau,' he exclaimed. 'When I heard you were moving up here with your pylons I was dismayed, for I thought you'd requisition my best grazing pastures. But lo and behold, thanks to providence you took barren rocky acres I hadn't got much use for anyway.'

'I expect,' said Tommy sagaciously, 'you had the Country Party to thank for the choice of land as well.'

'Now, now!' cried Julius. 'Not a word against the Country Party. The Nationalists may rule the country, and were I not a pastoralist, I admit I would personally support them. Meanwhile, there's the Labour Party trying to wreck us, and the good old Country Party, even if in a permanent minority, providing the solid core that keeps the country on an even keel.'

'Personally, I vote Labour,' said J G.

'No!' Julius cried, as might an honest woman happening on a harlot.

'And me Nationalist,' said Tommy. 'They've got the majority of the country's interests at heart, and don't forget I'm by birth a city man.'

'But J G, I'm astounded!' cried Julius again. '*You*, an educated responsible man, a supporter of the A L P?'

'Mr Macnamara, you must remember Tommy and I are not capitalists, or landowners, but technicians. And in my view, our interests coincide with those of the working-man.'

'In *my* view,' said Tommy, 'since the Australian workingman's the idlest bludger in the universe, either playing two-up or taking hour-long smoke-ohs when he should be toiling, my interests don't coincide with his, and that's why I'm a stalwart Nationalist.'

'But the A L P, J G! I'm shocked!'

'*Well*, Mr Macnamara . . . Nothing could be more shocking to me than the horse-trading the Country Party always does to get a few seats in the Federal cabinet.'

'But I *am* a horse trader, among other things, J G!' (This was considered funny, and got a laugh.) 'At all events, to tell you what's now, I suppose, an open secret, I mean to stand for this constituency in the Country Party interest next elections . . . And whatever your personal political affinities, I'm going to ask you to forget politics and remember friendship, and both register your votes for me. Cheerioh!'

'Cheers, Mr Macnamara!' said the engineers, both thinking, 'Not bloody likely, you old rogue.'

'What,' cried Julius, 'would agriculture be without technicians like yourselves? The development of this country is entirely due to the sweat of the agriculturalist, and the brains of the agricultural engineers. That's why I admire you both and make bold, despite your passing prejudices, to ask you to vote for me like all good associates and neighbours. Good gracious me!'

This was provoked by the abrupt appearance, wobbling slightly, of Mrs Baxter. For an instant Julius gazed at her like a boy caught stealing apples, but soon his red face became suffused with an air of injured, venomous resentment. 'Good gracious, Mrs Baxter!' he exclaimed, rising. 'Is anything amiss?'

Mrs Baxter seated herself with the strength of one who, with but one feeble card to play (in this case, that of common sense and old time's sake), and the determination to cut losses if it should be a loser, said slowly to Macnamara, 'No, no, nothing of that nature . . . It's just I was feeling a bit lonely, and feeling it was a long time too since I set eyes on dear Mrs Bailey. So that I changed my mind despite all my fatigue and decided to accept her kind invitation and pop over.'

'Ah, but Mrs Baxter!' said Julius, lowering himself again and manifestly dissatisfied with this. 'I'm going to ask these two good friends of mine to excuse me, because I *do* want to speak to you about something by ourselves for just an instant.'

'*We'll* go,' said J G Eaton. 'I must be back to my gramophone duty, anyway. Come along Tommy—you're not tripping the light fantastic nearly enough this evening. I know the bar's your favourite lurk, of course, but you do owe a duty to the young ladies.'

'Nice to see you, Mrs Baxter,' said Tommy, rather vague as to who she was. 'Could I get you another spot, if that's what your drinking?'

'That would be most cordial of you,' said Mrs Baxter like a dowager, and despite Julius's mounting and evident impatience.

When the drink was delivered, and the engineers had departed, Mrs Baxter cut short an angry opening of Julius's by saying, 'Just—one—moment!'

'What!?'

'In the first place, are you saying I am *not* invited here?'

'No, you always are, of course; but you don't usually care to come, and if you wanted to, why didn't you come earlier with me? Because turning up so late does look peculiar, especially as I haven't mentioned that you will . . .'

'Finished? So I *am* invited, Mr Macnamara?'

'I said you were: yes.'

'Good. Then that's all there is to be said, isn't it?'

Julius leaned forward. '*Far* from it, Mrs Baxter. There's a whole *lot* to be said between you and me.'

She beamed at him, to his intense annoyance. 'All right then,' she cried, '—say it. And I might have a little bit to say in return to you as well.'

'Why *have* you come?'

'Listen, now, Macnamara. Do you want the truth from me, or do you want a fable?'

'I want to know *why* you've come.'

Mrs Baxter lowered her hand-bag to the floor and placed two massive hands (still gloved) upon either massive knee. 'I've come,' she said positively, 'in a last probably vain attempt,

Macnamara, to preach some word of reason to you. Oh, no! Now, *you* listen just a moment! If I go, I go: back to the temperance hotel if they'll ever have me, or off to my married sister's down in Tassie. You've never given me enough to save, but I'm *not* so dependent on your whims and fancies as you imagine. *Your* trouble is, you know, you've gone too far. And that's what you're in danger of doing again, and that's why I've come to warn you.'

Torn between resentment that she was talking of leaving before *he* made her, and fear that she might know secrets that would upset his cherished, obsessive plans, Julius's face expressed anxiety, rage, and considerable sulks.

'So you see, my dear man,' she continued, waving her glass about, 'you've got nothing left to hold *me* by—unless you want to. And why you *should* want to is because I *do* understand you, and can put up with you . . .'

'You do *not* understand me! No one does!'

'Least of all yourself. And pardon *me*—I can put up with from you what nobody else in the wide world would. And of *all* persons the least likely to, is that young girl Nancy . . . '

'I refuse to . . .'

'Shut up! A girl who cares about as much for you as an abo hunter does for a fat old dugong!'

'Beware!' cried Julius, looking like Mephistopheles's uncle.

'Of what? What are *you* trying to scare me with?'

He looked at her darkly. 'Of the black side of my character, if you want to know, Mrs Baxter!'

'Haven't I seen plenty of that already? Look, Julius! Don't you understand . . .'

'You are *not* to call me Julius. That was agreed between us.'

'All agreements are now cancelled out, Macnamara. Just let me explain you to yourself. You're not a good man, you're just silly and you're evil. But because you're silly, you're weak, and your evil will never be effective . . . Least of all, Julius, on me, because I've seen far more evil down there in the city, and in my own past life, than you will ever understand or realize; and with all these years, I've learned to live with it, and prevent it, and not let it affect me.'

'I think you're drunk.'

'Oh yes—and so are you. But I'm drunk and speaking sense, and you're drunk and evading every issue.'

Julius rose. 'You have twenty-four hours,' he said with apoplectic dignity, 'to pack your bags and get your fat useless body off my property.'

'Fat? Useless? Take a look in the mirror sometime, Julius. You're going to destroy yourself playing with fire, I tell you! You're back in your boyhood, trying to tempt providence like a child. Well, providence is unforgiving to sinful men, and specially so when they should be old enough to know what they're doing. And providence will not forgive you, even if your poor body has its weaknesses! So *you* beware, Macnamara! *You* watch out you're not heading for damnation!' She pointed a thick gloved finger at him. 'Just think again: and if you want me —if you've got sense enough to change your foolish mind— *you*'ve still got twenty-four hours to save yourself from a whole heap of horrid misery.'

Julius threw her a regard of the utmost malevolence, slammed down his glass, and strode out hunching his shoulders spasmodically.

'Well, heigh-ho,' said Mrs Baxter to herself; and rising, she replenished her glass from the deserted bar and knocked back the liquor in one gurgling gulp. 'Heigh-ho—what a pity,' she continued pensively and out aloud. 'For I *could* be of service to him, even though it *is* to my own best material advantage.'

Here she sat solo, listening to the yells and music from the distant carnival, and meditating on her past, her present, and her doubtful future. 'The trouble is,' she announced to herself, 'I'm getting *old*. I'm in good shape—I mean this old body' (she

patted her corseted belly)—'but there's no doubt—oh dear!—
I'm all set now for my decline. Because when you cease to be
useful to *any*one—even to the worst of them—your life's really
over and done for. Oh, my lord! You did give me a turn!'

It was Helen, who had appeared in the darkness beyond the
light on the veranda. Once again, without wishing to, she had
made one of those 'entrances' which somehow never failed to be
sensational. 'Oh, did I scare you, Mrs Baxter? Please forgive
me! I was taking a little stroll in the cool to calm my nerves. But
gracious me, I haven't even said yet how glad and surprised I am
to see you. You don't come over to Cootamundra nearly enough
—I'm always asking Julius to bring you . . .'

'That's a little fib, now, isn't it, Mrs Bailey?'

'Oh *no*, it isn't. You know I've always liked you, and you
know I've called on you more than once at Macnamara's . . .'

'Called on *Mr* Macnamara . . .'

'I've been there, surely, when only you were . . .'   .

'And when you found *he* was out.'

'Oh, come, Mrs Baxter! You're surely not saying I am an
enemy, or anything of that description?'

'Do sit down, dear, you make me dizzy looking up at you like
this. There—that's better. No—of course not an enemy. I never
said you treat me like one—all I was trying to say was (and I'm
not *blaming* you, mark you) that you don't give a damn for me, in
point of fact.'

'Oh, Mrs Baxter!'

'Oh, Mrs Bailey, then!'

'Well!'—Helen gave her silvery laugh—'you're saying I'm
selfish—thoughtless—are you?'

'No . . . you are selfless and thoughtful when your own interest is involved . . .'

'But, Mrs Baxter! How can you say I don't do the best I can
in all the district . . .'

'Look, dear, you operate from strength, that's all I mean.

You've got looks, money, position and you use them beautifully when you feel inclined to.'

'You *are* making me out an unpleasant character, Mrs Baxter.'

'*Your* trouble, dear, is that you've got no character at all.'

'*I* haven't?'

'Well—no will, then.'

'But what *do* you know about me, dear Mrs Baxter, please?'

'Perhaps more than you do yourself. You live in a dream world, Helen Bailey. And your weakness is you can never make up your mind about a thing. You just drift through your days in this world like a piece of thistledown.'

'I admit I'm not *practical* . . .'

'Oh, I don't mean that you can't fit a nut onto a bolt, exactly. I just mean you don't know *what* you want, my dear.'

Helen, full of exalted thoughts of what she did at present most want in the entire world, found this untrue.

'You're unjust, Mrs Baxter, to me. You judge only by appearances. I have a rather . . . complicated nature, rather a sad one, and I suffer . . .'

'So do we all: that's why we have to seek for remedies.'

'Even for situations that have none?'

'If they have none, we leave them and try to find something better we can handle.'

Helen brushed fair hair away from her forehead with a wayward finger. 'Mrs Baxter,' she said, 'are you perhaps referring . . . to what's painful and private to me (oh, God knows it's painful and, because it is so, must be private) . . . to my marriage?'

'Yep.'

Helen, the non-drinker, went to the bar, filled up two glasses, and returned to her interlocutor.

'Mrs Baxter,' she said, 'I have three alternatives, and only three. To go, to stay and suffer, and to hope. And I cannot go because I dearly hope . . .'

'Now just a minute, dearie . . .'

'You think if I left Cootamundra I'd be destitute. You think I depend on being here? Don't you know that if I *did* go, my husband, like a gentleman, would see to it I didn't starve and that he'd never divorce me? All this is hard for me to say to you, Mrs Baxter: but I say it because you tell me I run away from facts if I can't bear them.'

'But you *do* depend on Cootamundra.'

'You mean on the *comfortable* life here? Oh, if only you knew!'

'No. I mean you depend on the *un*comfortable life here. What you feel you want, Mrs Bailey—and believe me, I'm not being catty, I've no reason for it—what you want is to hang on year by year *never* making any decision! That's been your whole life!'

Helen's face grew hard: and when it did this rarely, her countenance really was transformed: revealing the severity that weakness feels when the props and supports to its self-assurance are endangered.

'I do think, Mrs Baxter, you're being highly inconsiderate and unwise. My life with Walter has not been a simple one, and no one who does not know it fully can attribute blame.' Her mind cleared by the rejection of the other woman's attacking, subversive notions, there flooded into it her dear image of Norman; and once again Helen was transformed.

'But never mind, Mrs Baxter!' she cried. 'We're all here to enjoy ourselves this evening—each and every one of us—and surely the whole point of a party is to forget our troubles for an instant and live for what joy the passing moment can bring us as a gift.'

On this exit line she rose, and at this critical juncture (as might have been expected) she was rescued by the entrance of J G Eaton, carrying records, and crying, 'A slow tango, Mrs Bailey! A slow tango, and I've promised myself I'd ask *you* to teach it to me so as I can match up with Margaret when she comes! Besides, I've had enough for the moment of being master of ceremonies, and Tommy has taken over on the gramophone. He's going to play this, and I've asked him to give us repeat performances of it till I get the hang of the steps from you to a T. Come along, *s'il vous plaît, madame.* It's a slow dance, so I shan't stumble over your feet despite my defective eyesight.'

And holding out his arm—and she taking it gaily and desperately—he led her to the uproarious saloon. On the way she said, 'Why do you *still* call me "Mrs Bailey" always, J G? I've never been so aloof as to call you "Mr Eaton".'

'Mrs Bailey,' he said, pausing on the noisy threshold, 'I admire and respect you too much ever to call you by the title of that illustrious goddess of ancient Greece whose glamorous name you bear! Now: what do I do with my feet—or should we have a drink to set us up before you are gracious enough to demonstrate all the intricacies?'

She positioned herself and him—in that classic, and slightly ludicrous Latin-American pose—and as the music began, they glided into the ad hoc ballroom laced together. Since the tango was too much for many of the dancers, they had the floor mostly to themselves: and great was the admiration of Helen's poise, and great the amusement at J G's series of steps which caricatured the Argentinian bounder.

'I'm getting it! I'm getting it!' he cried, as he leaned over her like an anglo-saxon gigolo.

'Hold me up, J G, or you'll have us both over!' his alarmed hostess exclaimed.

'Won't Margaret be delighted with me when she sees me performing this . . . oops, sorry, Mrs Bailey, I'm all feet—sees me gallivanting in this voluptuous dago manner? I can't wait for her to behold me—I can't wait, for that matter, to behold her! Because I love her, Mrs Bailey, from the bottom of my worthless heart. Ah, love! (sorr-y!—let's try again!) Ah, as I was saying—love! It certainly makes the world go round, and I don't mind telling you, Mrs Bailey, that my love for Margaret—and hers, yes hers, for me!—are such that Romeo and Juliet, and Dante and that other woman's will be as nothing beside the pair of us! Oh, Mrs Bailey! Just wait till you see the one and only Margaret! And just wait till you see the happiness of J G and Mrs Margaret Eaton!'

Helen halted. 'If you don't stop talking,' she cried out, 'and if you don't stop telling me about Margaret, I shall *scream*.' And she ran out of the room leaving J G stumbling in amazement on the flour-encrusted ballroom floor.

The tango of Norman and Nancy was certainly sexually more successful . . . in fact several of the older men, however tolerant, thought they were overdoing it a bit. 'Take it easy, son,' said Nancy, pressing up against him, 'or you'll do yourself some injury.'

'On you, more than likely . . . you want to come outside?'

'No thanks—I've had my ration for today . . . You can save all that for when we're both bottled up at Macnamara's.' The tango scratched to a languishing, syncopated stop. 'Well—what about Maureen: you won your bet from me yet?'

Norman eyed her. 'Third time lucky,' he replied. 'I'll report back before midnight—wait and see!'

Maureen, handing records to Tommy Mulligan, observed Norman with contempt and envy. 'God, that boy, he needed his pants taking down and whipping! Who *did* he think he was, behaving like the Son of the Sheikh in public!'

'One day that boy will go too far,' said Tommy Mulligan, also eyeing Norman with highest disapproval. 'One day he'll meet a man who'll *show* him where he belongs. Or more likely a woman who'll make him suffer a bit and break his bloody heart—if he's got one.'

'He needs controlling, but he needs love,' said Maureen, rallying, despite herself, to his defence.

'He needs *what*?' cried Tommy . . . but her answer was lost in the resonant tinklings of the two-step.

'Not dancing?' said Julius in her ear as he passed by. 'Picking and choosing as usual, I suppose. Well, my dear, don't pick and choose too long . . . An old bachelor may seem ridiculous to you, but to most of us there's nothing more contemptible than a woman who blows hot and cold and ends up with nothing at all . . .'

She looked at him, then said, 'I hear you've arranged poor old Nance won't end up with nothing at all.'

'And not only Nancy, may I tell you! Others will come to Macnamara's and be lost to you! Here, Norman!' cried the pastoralist commandingly, beckoning the boy. 'Why don't you ask this lonely young lady for a dance?'

'A pleasure,' said Norman bowing with stiff solemnity—Pommie-style, as he imagined it.

Maureen hesitated, then took Tommy's arm. 'Come on,' she said, 'you can leave that machine to J G now, and have this one with me.'

Smiling unpleasantly, Norman made for the bar outside and in the doorway was halted by the massive form of Mrs Baxter. 'You chose the wrong one to dance with, son,' she said, 'and the one you should have chosen wouldn't even look at you.'

'And who might you be, old lady,' Norman said, 'when you're at home?'

'You'll find out soon enough,' said Mrs Baxter, accepting the offer of a waltz from an elderly veterinary doctor.

Norman shrugged, got his drink, drained it, poured another, and walked out across the veranda onto the buffalo grass, crisp and luminous beneath the moon. Away through the trees he could see the lights from Walter Bailey's annexe (where Walter was polishing, polishing that repeating rifle, then writing in his diary, then polishing, polishing again), and across the plain he saw glowing the red lights on the eight summits of the radio towers. He smiled in the night at the recollection of his climb the evening before, then frowned at the effrontery of the girl

Maureen . . . then grimaced with revulsion at the memory of Nancy (there was never *anything* in easy girls: but then, all girls were easy!): but he started and stopped when a voice from the ghost-gums called to him, 'Norman, oh Norman,—come and be with me!'

*

Helen held out her arms to him like the eternal mother-lover, and enfolded him, greatly to his surprise. And embarrassment indeed, for he was not sure how to take this . . . was it tender and affectionate, as his own mum might have been, or was it an older woman asking him to come on? But the night's cloak gave him assurance (even if the doubt persisted), and he returned her kisses with reserved enthusiasm. She took his hand, and started running through the wattles (hell!—she knows the way, I don't, thought Norman as the boughs whipped and scratched his face) till they came to the open land beyond the plantations, and stood gazing out across the flat prairie, whose huge rocks—and occasional shuffling animals—were caught by the glancing light from overhead. To the left lay the big dam like a sheet of golden silver.

After a silent pause Norman said, 'You don't mind if we sit down a minute, Helen? To tell you the truth, you've pumped all the breath out of my poor carcase.'

Without answering, she pulled him down beside her, and they sat shoulder to shoulder holding hands. Then Helen—whose pale face he could barely discern, but whose scent was present and commanding—turned to him and said in a low voice, 'I love you, Norman Culley.'

He was completely taken aback. 'You *love* me, Helen? But what does that mean?'

'Just that I love you, Norman'—and she caressed his cheek lingeringly and ran her hand over his neck and hair.

'Well—well, I say, thanks, Mrs Bailey. But now—well,

Helen—when you say *love*, what exactly had you got in mind?'

'In *mind*, Norman? Love needs no explanation.'

'No? Well, look—look, Helen, perhaps we've got different ideas about explaining it.'

'And what are yours?'

'Mine? Matter of fact, it's not a word I often use. Of course, if a sheila says, "Do you love me, Norman?" or some such palaver, I always answer, yes I do. But that's only because . . . well, look, Helen—ought we to be talking about all this?'

'Only because you want to possess her?'

'Eh? Yeah. That's it—if I want to possess her. That's my idea of love!'

She laughed: 'You poor boy!'

'What's so poor about me, Helen?'

'Oh, of course love is possession! But not only of the body— of the heart, the mind, the spirit, the whole being!'

'Now, look! Helen, those are only words!'

'Words have a meaning in our lives . . .'

'Maybe they do, but by love I understand . . . well, having a girl, but that's all there is to it, and there's nothing else so far as I'm concerned.'

She kissed him again. 'I see I must teach you, Norman.'

'Teach me what?'

She moved away a bit, though still holding both his hands, and said, 'All my life, Norman, I have been possessed of a great secret, a great knowledge. I have known it as a child, a girl, a married woman—always. And it is that we are born into this world to fulfil our lives by fulfilling that of someone else. And what we give to him is *every*thing—everything we possess . . . our hearts, our bodies, our last farthing . . . something single, absolute and entire.'

'And . . . what do you get back in return?'

'The same fulfilment.'

'And you, Helen: you've had this in your life?'

'Oh, no. Only, so far, in my faith and my imagination.'

'Yeah. Well, Helen, frankly, if this is love, haven't you waited a long time for it?'

'Ah, yes: I have. But there I made one fatal mistake . . . one terrible error of judgement. My feeling was not wrong—what I longed to give, and longed for in return—but my choice of the man with whom I could make this splendid exchange which would create us both, was not the right one. Do not think I am blaming my husband, Norman—Walter Bailey. People think up here I married him for money: I did not. I had many offers when a girl, even what were known as more advantageous. But in Walter I saw the man who I believed to be the one to whom I should give, and from whom I could receive. And though from the beginning—and even throughout years (years of great pain to me, Norman)—I could not meet his heart, nor he mine, as I had hoped to (and as he, too, I believe, has hoped), yet the faith —an eternal faith—has remained in me *till today* that one day— oh! one precious glorious day!—we would be together as one single person.'

'Till today, you say. Could it be, Helen, you mean that's where I come in?'

'Yes: from the moment of seeing you I knew my error was over, and that you were the man I could give to what is most precious to me, and who in return, could give this joy to me.'

'But why *me*, Helen! Gawd, look! You scarcely know me!'

'Oh yes, I do . . . I've known you for nearly forty years.'

'But—here! You made a mistake with Mr Bailey . . .'

'I was younger: now I know my heart completely.'

Norman took away his hands, brought out a handkerchief, and wiped his nose. 'Look, Helen,' he said again. 'Please believe me I admire you and respect you like few women I've yet met, and few I've known such a very short while as you. But honest, as I see it, I'm useless to you—well, just look at me! My age, my background, no money—I mean nothing you're looking for whatever. And besides . . .'

'*Yes*, Norman?'

'Well, this word "love", as you understand it. I don't think I *love* you like that, Helen, at all, or ever could do. In fact I don't think I really know what you mean by all those words and notions . . . No, no, don't misunderstand me. I'm not contradicting you . . . all this may be real to you, or just real—I couldn't say. But it doesn't make sense to me, Helen, you've got to believe me.'

'Time will teach you, Norman. I shall be patient, now I am so sure.'

Norman, though enormously fascinated—and even flattered—by this unexpected episode (quite outside his experience, and there was no denying Helen was a *remarkable* woman—far more so than any who'd yet noticed him—even if she did seem at times a trifle dotty), began nevertheless to feel himself hemmed in, oppressed . . . almost captured by all this extraordinary vehemence; and an instinct of self-preservation surged into his being. 'Helen,' he said. 'Don't you really feel you ought to think over all this a bit?' (The classic words of the older to the younger!). 'I'm going home tomorrow, and I won't be in the area again till I'm not sure when, so don't you think you ought to wait and see if I mean anything to you when I'm out of sight?'

'As long as I live, I shall love you, Norman. As long as I live, I shall never forget you for an instant.'

'Oh, look, Helen,—really!'

'Yes, Norman—really!' She kissed him again gently, without demanding, but with a confident possession. 'You were sent to me, Norman,' she said. 'And having waited so long I shall not be impatient, knowing so surely you will return to me because only through me can you be fulfilled.'

Norman didn't like this bit much. 'What does *that* mean, Helen?' he asked her.

'There is a wonder in you, Norman, that you do not yet know. You are no ordinary man: you are a hero, a . . .'

'Hey, Helen! Now look: I'm *not* a hero . . .'

'. . . a hero, Norman, doesn't mean only brave, but a man born with greatness in him, and I can show this greatness to you— reveal to you the glory in yourself you do not know . . .'

'Now, honest, Helen: this is all a bit over my head. I know I've got qualities, and I've confidence in myself and my abilities, but I don't think I'm all that exceptional . . . even though I do find a lot of young fellers of my age are dopes . . .'

'You will see,' she said calmly, with assurance.

'I want to get *on*, of course,' he said. 'I want to make my way and *mean* something. I want to *win*: and I'm ready to work for that, to sacrifice myself. But for that I'll need time, and I'll need money.'

'Your youth gives you time. Money will come to you. Everyone will give it to you . . . I will, if you wish.'

'You will? Money?'

'Yes.'

The thought crossed Norman's mind that she was trying to buy his favours, yet he instantly dismissed it. 'Helen, this is ever so decent of you, but I *can* make my own way, and I will.'

'And I can give you love, Norman, such as you've never known from anyone else and never will.'

'Helen, I really am getting a bit confused. Do you mean you want me to . . . I mean here . . . now . . . is that what you want from me?'

'Only when you want it yourself with me, Norman: now: tomorrow: any day of your life and mine till I must die, as I will, before you, and you set out, a man I have revealed to himself, to conquer the whole world!'

Highly perplexed, he gave her a hesitant kiss. 'It's very sweet of you, you know, but honestly I don't feel we ought to do anything like that just now . . .'

125

'Because of my husband?'

Fuck your husband, Norman thought, but said, 'No, no, because—well, see it this way, Helen. It's not just that you're older
than me, or anything like that, or that I don't like you, because I
do, it's just that . . . well, see, it wouldn't really be suitable.'

'Why?'

Norman hesitated. Could he talk her out of all this and get her
back to the house, he wondered? Or should he keep quiet, give
her a go—and would that satisfy her? Or should he . . . and now
he felt he'd *have* to say it, because he sensed this woman was
immensely serious about something he could hardly understand.

'Because, Helen,' he said, 'I could never make love with you
when there's another person here I really . . . well, to use your
word, I'd say I love her.'

There was an enormous silence. 'And who is that?' said
Helen.

'Well—it's Maureen.'

'Oh.'

Helen sat quiet for all of four minutes till Norman began to
feel alarmed. 'Yes—I'm very keen on Maureen . . . I mean really
keen,' he said.

'Oh.' Helen rose to her feet and Norman got up slowly too, and
stood before her in the moonlight.

'So *go* with Maureen,' said Helen softly. 'Go take your love,
and I will know that what I've hoped to give, I've given, and
what I hoped to receive, I may not do.'

She said this with such intensity that Norman feared tears,
hysteria, he knew not what. He leant over to kiss her and she received this calmly, and returned it as if aloof from him altogether.

'So Helen . . . shouldn't we get back just now . . . don't you
think they'll miss us . . . ?'

'I shall stay here by myself awhile.'

'You certain?'

'Yes.'

The moon flickered behind a stray fleeting cloud, and they heard the sound of a night rabbiter's distant gun.

'Well, so long for now, then,' said Norman awkwardly. He moved off, hands in his shorts' pockets, then turning, said, 'Look! Here's a little keepsake for you. What my old mum used to call a memento'—and he handed her the opal Maureen had given to him. It blinked at Helen as the moon emerged serenely in the dazzling Australian sky.

✶

The shot was from Walter Bailey's gun, and had failed to kill him: failed because, in the last split second, his face was quicker than his thumb, and he'd jerked the gun out of his mouth before he pulled the trigger. As it was, the bullet had burned the side of his head and imbedded itself in the chest of an ancestral Bailey behind him, depicted in a framed oleograph. He had waited to see if anyone came running, but the noise at the house was too violent, and he was left alone, trembling, and fortifying himself from a brandy bottle.

'Well,' he said to himself, 'I've got that over once and for all. I mean the attempt: I know now it fascinates me no longer, and I'll never ever try to do it again.'

He had weighed up the pros and cons all evening. In favour of death there seemed the idea that his life had become quite mean-ingless, and that he had waited too long, and too patiently, for it ever to change. In favour, too, was the thought that he would free Helen, though he also guessed how much she depended on his silent presence, and how grievously his departure would disturb her. In favour again that, in this most momentous moment of all, the decision as to the means and moment of his death would be his and his alone. But against it all his conscience had spoken of cowardice, and even more of the *vanity* there would be in sup-posing anyone would be as interested in this event—or shocked by it—as he himself would. If only one could kill oneself and then, so to speak, live to see what happened! Walter reflected, as he downed more brandy. And he realized it had been, in that precious, precarious split second, the thought of the *absurdity*—the lack of dignity—of his act, that had halted him at death's door.

He looked at his diary and recalled—as if it were a hundred years ago—that he had written as his final entry:

> Still no rain: but the barometer suggests a possibility, so have cleaned out and prepared the rain-gauges for any downfall.

*

As he reached the house, headlamps dazzled Norman, he backed on to the verge, and the car pulled up. It was Mrs Baxter's runabout, and sitting next to her he saw Maureen.

'And where are you off to?' Norman asked, leaning possessively on the window.

'Mrs Baxter's going home, and I'm opening the first gate for her.'

'Before I get too blotto, son, I thought I'd better be making tracks.'

'I'll hop in the dickey and walk you back,' said Norman.

'If you care to. Okay, Mrs Baxter, I think he's in.'

'Well, there you are, my dear,' said Mrs Baxter, manœuvring the winding drive expertly. 'And don't forget: I'll be leaving the district all too soon for the capital, but if there's anything I can do for you before I go, you've only got to tell me.'

'Thanks, Mrs Baxter. You never know in this world, do you.'

'You don't indeed, dear. And a friend in need is indeed a friend indeed.'

Norman manipulated the gates, and they bid Mrs Baxter a

rousing farewell. 'As for you,' were her last words to Norman, 'don't forget however smart you may be, there's always someone smarter. That's what *I*'ve found, anyway, to my cost, so you might as well pay attention to a wise old woman's words even though she's had too many.'

They waved her away, and watched and listened as the lights narrowed on the prairie, and the motor became a rising-falling whine. Then they stood a moment embarrassed, till they took hands because this was the night, and this was the convention, and after all they did like each other even though neither had yet shown or told this in an acceptable way.

They started back up the track with the slow speed of reluctance, and all of a sudden Maureen halted underneath the stars. Around them lay the total silence of the sub-tropical night: so large, so vast a silence that it seemed to echo.

'Tell me, Norman Culley,' she said. 'Why is it you are such a bastard when I really believe you're quite a decent sort of a boy?'

'And *you* tell me, Maureen, why you always try to make me feel small, and act like you're Norma Talmadge, and yet make it clear, somehow, you do care for me a bit?'

'I'll *tell* you, son. Because you take too much for granted.'

'I admit I do. All *right*. Maureen, I love you, can I give you a kiss?'

'You *love* me? You *do* take me for Norma Talmadge!'

'You don't believe in love, then?'

'I'll tell you when you've done what you said you wanted to.'

It was extraordinary, thought Norman, how when you kissed a sheila, whatever her height, if you *liked* her, and she liked you, your two heights seemed to match up exactly! And it was extraordinary, thought Maureen, how a tough larrikin like Norman could feel so soft and gentle when you got up really close to him and he behaved.

'So you don't believe in love!' said Norman, standing away in front of her.

'Oh, that's only for film stars, like I said. All I can understand is boy meets girl—*provided*,' Maureen added with great emphasis, 'it *is* boy meets girl, and not boy acts like a giddy galoot and thinks the sheila's coming to him running just because he's so bloody marvellous.'

He kissed her again. 'Well, I believe in love a bit, you know . . .' he said quietly. 'I mean if you could *find* the sheila . . . one who wanted to *give* you a bit, not just take and *use* you like they all do . . .'

'So they all do?'

'You want me to say, "all except you", Maureen?'

'Well, try saying it.'

'Okay, I'll say it: you *give*, don't you, you don't only take . . . And if you do that, then I can give to you . . .'

'I know I'm going to take another kiss from you . . .'

'Well, let's make this a real film stars' one! Cameras!' cried Norman to the night, as he kissed her everywhere and let his hands roam without resistance.

Maureen was now waiting for the *moment* that Gawd knows she'd longed for, and Gawd knows she was ready to give without scruple provided the feller acted right . . . but somehow this strange kid, Norman, now he had the chance she'd so long wanted—and thought he surely did—was only feeling her, just like the kids back home had done in childhood when they used to play at 'doctors'.

'Yes, I *do* love you, Maureen,' said Norman as if to himself, 'and you know what you're going to do?'

('This is it,' thought Maureen.)

'You're going to marry me, and come with me up to Queensland, and I'm not going to stay in this bloody state any longer, even though I have had offers.'

He withdrew from her a moment, though still holding her hands, and said, 'You going to be Mrs Culley, for me, are you Maureen?'

'You serious?'

'I've asked you . . .'

'You mean Mrs *Norman* Culley?'

'Mrs Maureen, wife of Norman, Culley—yes: you're on?'

'The stars are our witness, Norman,' she said, gazing up at the Southern Cross. 'They see all and protect the true and rebuke the faithless, so my old ma says.'

'Then it's all signed and settled,' said Norman, kissing her again.

But still he only kissed her, and Maureen felt something was *wrong* about all this, and felt somehow that an alien presence was hovering over Norman which might steal him from her, so still holding his hands she lay down on the tussocks pulling him after her, and wrapped herself round him till she felt his whole being was to be given to her alone. 'You're teaching me love,' he whispered into her hair, 'I'm learning about love today . . .'

'You teach me, Norman,' she said, forgetting the whole world except for Norman and Maureen in this moment.

★

But Walter's shot at himself had not passed unheard: for J G Eaton, though his sight was weak, had caught with sharp ears the distant report above the blaring of the gramophone; and leaving the instrument to Tommy he set off, vaguely uneasy, to confirm or dismiss an instinct he had that the shot might have come from the annexe.

Peering through the uncurtained window, his suspicions were aroused by seeing Walter putting a rifle away among the other weapons in his gun-rack. So he tapped on the pane, and when Walter swung abruptly round, cried, 'It's only me—J G Eaton,' through the glass.

Walter did not open the door, but the window, and said to J G (as J G thought, in a manner more guilty than annoyed), 'What is it, Mr Eaton? Why have you left the festivities?'

'I thought I heard a shot from down this way.'

'You were correct: you did: I was cleaning my rifle, and it went off accidentally.'

Because of his eyesight, and because Walter's back was to the light, J G could not confirm, or otherwise, the truth of this from a sight of Walter's face; yet though the tone was decisive, J G didn't quite credit what he heard. (Guns do *not* go off 'accidentally' in experienced hands.)

'And you're sure you're all right? No damage was done, Mr Bailey?'

'Only,' said Walter, waving at the oleograph on the wall, 'to this memorial of my ancestor.'

J G peered and continued, 'So there's nothing I can do for you?'

Walter paused, then said—prompted by some mysterious telepathy—'But is my wife all right, Eaton?'

'Your wife? She wasn't down here, was she?'

'I think she is somewhere near . . . I fancy so . . .'

'Really? Well, if you're sure you're okay, Mr Bailey, I'll go and make sure that all is well with her too.'

Walter nodded, closed the window, and turned out the light; bemused, J G set off again along the path towards the house when, emerging into a moonlit clearing of the buffalo-grass lawn, he saw and heard a truly surprising sight: of Helen Bailey on her knees, clasping Maureen's, and Norman vainly trying to disengage her and raise her up, and Helen crying, 'Oh, have pity Maureen! For he means so much more to me than he can ever do to you!'

At the view of J G, all three actors in this tableau froze: until Helen leapt up, uttered a short cry, and ran past J G through the wattle towards the clearing beside the big dam that led out onto the wide prairie beyond.

'But what is amiss?' J G cried, advancing on the young pair.

Maureen said nothing, and Norman answered, 'Helen's had a bit of a nervous crisis, I should say.'

'You call her Helen?'

'Isn't that her name?'

'But what *has* happened, Maureen? And where's she gone?'

'To the radio station,' Maureen said quietly.

'To the *radio station*? But why? How?'

'She said if I didn't do as she asked she'd climb up the mast and throw herself off it.'

'*Helen* said what? Said that?'

'I've told you: if I didn't do what she wanted; but I couldn't.'

'And you mean she's going there now? Then we must stop her car down at the gate!'

'She won't be going in her car: she'll run there across the paddocks.'

'*Run* there? All those miles? What *is* happening, Maureen? Norman! Culley! What *is* happening?'

'She's had a sort of a dizzy spell—she seems all excited and hysterical.'

'But we must stop her: where's Tommy? We must get out the cars and stop her . . . Norman! Maureen! Are you *serious*?'

'I think,' Norman said, 'that Mrs Bailey does want to kill herself.'

Galvanized into action, J G rushed to the house and imparted his confused message to Tommy Mulligan. The agitation of the two engineers communicated itself to the assembly, and soon a confusion erupted in the house, as if its focal point, its centre of gravity, its very meaning had suddenly been desecrated and lost. One of the first to catch the vague anxious drift of what the engineers were talking about, Julius listened carefully, frowned inwardly, examined his troubled soul, and sought out Nancy. 'My dear,' he said to her, 'if you've decided to come with me, now's the time to do it.'

'You're eloping with me, Julius?' said the girl, fingering the chain that suspended his watch into a top pocket from his lapel.

'Nothing so strange as that, but a disaster is impending, and I think you and I had best be away from it to the safety of Macnamara's.'

She took his two large rounded shoulders, and gazed at him as if at a specimen of something: 'So you're going to be serious about me, old Julius Macnamara?' she said to him.

'As serious as I can be, Nancy, my dear. As serious as may be.'

'Me too I'll be serious, I'm telling you once and for all,' she said, then took his fat hand and the pair made their way to the garages whence, shortly afterwards, they departed from Cootamundra in the sprung comfort of Julius's slightly dated limousine.

Round the garages the confusion mounted of cars backing, turning, lights glaring, shouts, blowings of horns and occasional bumps and curses. Tommy Mulligan decided he'd try to follow Helen direct across the paddocks, to pick her up in his head-lamps, only making his way down to the gates whenever he should reach a wall or fence. J G, who wanted to follow him, was commanded by Tommy, because of his eyesight and inexperience behind the wheel, to follow the main track and try to make contact with Tommy at the gates. Other visitors, more or less inaccurately appraised of what was happening, departed in wrong directions, very intoxicated, insistently in search of they were not quite sure what.

'And what shall *we* do?' said Norman. 'Which lot shall we go with?'

'We'll go alone,' Maureen said. 'Can you drive her Armstrong-Siddeley?'

'I can drive anything.'

'Come on then—we'll take it, and try to track her like Tommy's doing across the paddocks.'

'Try to track her? You speak like this was a hunt,' cried Norman, starting up the big heavy car.

'It *is* a hunt,' Maureen answered. 'It's a hunt to save Mrs

Bailey from doing what would be useless to her. We must find her, Norman, and get her back to Cootamundra, where it's the only safe place for her to belong.'

*

Helen ran like the wind that was rising, perhaps presaging the rain. So often had she ridden out this way on horseback that she knew all the hills and gullies of the home paddocks, the last acres to the end of Bailey's, and the radio land that used to be Macnamara's out beyond. She did not choose to run because her brain was not clear enough to think of taking a car (or even a horse)—for indeed her brain was horribly clear, and precise, and certain. No, what she craved for was the sense of personal movement, speed, *involvement* with the night and air and bush so that *they*, as much as her racing feet, would carry her across the paddocks to her destiny. For Helen was not to kill herself only by despair: she was to do it, she knew, because it was at last revealed to her that if all she had dreamed of ever was to be utterly denied, to die was the destiny which she had not completely understood until the moment of seeing Norman with Maureen.

And so she sped on, a solitary figure in the great Australian night: tearing, stumbling, climbing, then coasting like a bird down shallow hills. At distances lights shone from time to time—behind her, to the side, sometimes in front, as if there were interfering persons searching for her; but she did not heed them, and barely deflected from her path knowing full well, as she did, that nothing could now come between her person and her purpose.

And the stars were enormous overhead, and enormous was the territory on which her feet (for her shoes soon fell away) were treading, of the vast, inhospitable, welcoming Australian continent: so welcoming, indeed, precisely because so disdainful of mankind . . . accepting his microbe presence because of its very millennial indifference to all that was not infinitely old. So old, that the modern Alpine Storms of younger continents had never torn its timeless calm, so ancient that there still wandered on its surface the last surviving children of pre-history. This old, doomed country that accepted you but never greeted, that could not hate you because it never loved or missed you, with its dim turgid consciousness of being in itself so eternal that nature's renewals of the plants, animals and human creatures were but the incident that scarcely caused to the huge continent more than the vestige of a weary antique sigh.

As her breath grew shorter, and her drenched body recovered, through movement, all its sense of being, Helen no longer felt agony, but exaltation. All her life she knew she had been consecrated to a great moment, and who could deny that to find the love she had sought and, seeing it was forbidden her, decide this moment of truth would also be her last, was not a fine, a splendid, honourable way for her to confirm that she had lived all her life faithful to her total belief in absolutes?

No, in this last hour she had no *blame* for anybody—not for her parents who bore her to this destiny, nor for Walter who had deceived her, nor for Maureen who had despoiled her, nor even for Norman who had not risen to the heights of being that only one such as she—exalted and entire—could ever attain. Nor did she blame herself for any fault . . . for had she not been always true to herself and her obsession—had she not supported every pain for years and declined both the compromises others made, and the drugged healing that comes from mere acceptance and the surrender to growing old? 'No!' she cried out to the warm wild lonely night, and to the stars. 'I have been Helen: I *am* Helen; and as Helen I shall always be remembered!'

The masts suddenly loomed nearer and she could descry, as she ran panting, the graceful lattice of their girders as they rose, so sure, elegant, lofty and potent, towards the sky. At the foot of the first one she reached she paused, gazed all around on her native land and its millions of square miles, and let the wind

wave in her hair, scented with the unforgettable dry-sweet tang
of eucalyptus and of wattle gum. She held out her arms beneath
the mast and the moon riding over it, and with tears of joy and
fulfilment in her eyes said, 'Oh yes, then, yes, good-bye!' Then
she began her climb up the narrow ladder that rose hundreds of
feet towards the stars. Half way up she looked down to earth and
was not frightened; though noticed that the mast seemed to
shrink to a narrow point at its concrete base just as, up above, it
narrowed once more to the summit where the huge cross-mast
extended on either side of the central column from a square
metal platform eight hundred feet up.

*

The first to see her, strangely enough, was Nancy—or to see
something up there on the mast—as Julius took the turn leading
down the valley to Macnamara's. Peering through the night she
said to him she thought she saw someone up there on the platform waving to the moon. Julius slowed down to walking pace,
gazed piercingly, then said, 'It may be an optical illusion, dear,
or it may be a person from the radio station carrying out some
sort of an examination; at all events, it's not our concern, I
wouldn't say, besides which you must be tired and I believe it's
going to rain.'

'Okay, me for a noggin at the homestead,' Nancy said, as they
accelerated into the darkness of the vale.

The next, as surprisingly, was J G Eaton: whose eyes, if near-
useless from close to, could in fact observe long distances; and
who, having the thought of Norman's exploit in his mind, had—
as if, perhaps also telepathically—glanced up to the platform
and seen *something*. He blew on his horn to Tommy, they made
for the last gate and hastened over towards the mast. Then, hearing the horns and the racings of two engines, Norman sped for
the track in the huge Armstrong-Siddeley, so that he and

Maureen joined the anxious party converging at the base of the tall tower.

'Let's have the lights out!' cried Tommy, 'so as I can see up there.' And walking backward out into the paddock, he gazed up aloft and cried out—rather absurdly—'Coo-ee!—are you up there Helen?'

A faint call like a song could be heard closer to the stars. Tommy ran back to the cars. 'It's her all right,' he cried. 'I'm going up.'

'No, me,' Norman shouted, approaching the base of the ladder. 'Oh, if only my eyes . . .' J G bewailed earnestly.

Tommy pulled Norman away, gave him a great shove into J G's arms, and started climbing steadily up the mast. His intoxicated head grew clearer as he rose, and youth returned to his muscles as he fulfilled the splendid destiny that—even today—survives in the Australian male as in few others, which is the absolute—and fully accepted—duty of succouring a fellow creature in any crisis of danger and of total need. Half way up he paused for breath, looked down at the upturned faces, then up at the gap by which the ladder entered the metal platform. Then shouting down, 'Okay so far,' and up, 'I'll be with you, Helen,' he climbed on in the night till he emerged onto the square of level steel, slightly swaying in the wind. There was no sign of Helen; and his heart missed a beat or two until he saw her standing on the cat-walk that ran on to the great transverse beam: holding a girder with one hand, and reaching out the other like a queen waving gently to the populace. 'Holy Christ!' said Tommy, now for the first time scared.

Helen saw him, and turned: at ease, apparently, on this precarious perch (that would have turned most heads). She looked at him calmly as he began threading his way, gingerly but with purpose, along the cat-walk in her direction. She made no movement, no anticipated threat. 'Oh, it's you, Tommy,' she said simply as he came within earshot of her.

He approached, and stopped prudently four or five feet away. 'I've come to fetch you, Helen,' he said quietly. 'You and I, you know, we're going to have a little chat and then go down.'

'No, Tommy. I've not come up here to go down again.'

'No? Well, you don't mind my talking to you, do you? Even up here in this a weird sort of a place?'

(Tommy was really doing well, for to tell the truth, he was now petrified—not only that he might have to grab her if she jumped, but even because—unexpectedly—he found himself horribly giddy all of a sudden.)

'Talk to me, Tommy, if you wish. But what is there left to say when I've come this far?'

'Only this, Helen. I want you to reflect, whatever you may have decided hitherto. Some of us are defeated, you know, and we just have to accept this and live on.'

'Why?'

'I don't know: as witnesses of our own failure, I suppose.'

'Why should we witness that?'

'To show we are brave. To show others we just must go on.'

'Why should we show them that?'

'I don't know, Helen. Do please come to the platform now with me, taking your time.'

She was silent a moment, then: 'You loved Nancy, Tommy.'

'Yes: I told you.'

'And you've lost her?'

'You know so.'

'And you want to live, to be a *witness* and to *show* people?'

Now he was silent in the wind. 'Oh no, Helen. All that's just nonsense: I want to live because I want to live. No other life is worth the loss of our own.'

'You believe that?'

'Yes.'

'Then you've never loved.'

'Take pity on me, then, Helen, and make me happy by coming down.'

'No, Tommy. It's my choice, my life, my destiny.'

She stood poised. Tommy had an inspiration. 'All right, Helen,' he said. 'But how am I to break this to your husband?'

'To Walter?'

'Won't this perhaps kill him too?'

'Walter? You don't know him: he's like iron.'

'Helen: J G thinks he tried to shoot himself tonight.'

'Is this true?'

'J G is truthful, Helen.'

'Kill himself? Why?'

'Oh, Helen: mustn't it be because of you?'

She held a cross-girder with each hand and faced him. 'Because of me? I mean something to him?'

'Don't you think you do?'

'Yes ... that is true ... I do think I do.'

'Then you have no right, Helen, to kill him as well as yourself ...'

The wind fell and there was a faint spit of drizzle in the air (or was it a night mist at this height?).

'All right, Tommy,' she said. 'Walk backwards, please, don't turn, and I'll follow you.'

'You promise? You don't want me to take your hand?'

'No ... all of a sudden I feel giddy: keep talking to me, Tommy.'

He walked back slowly and, as if in a trance, she followed him. As he felt the platform he paused, reached suddenly forward and grabbed her and she fainted into his arms.

He laid her on the serrated metal, hung firmly onto her ankle, and yelled down through the gap where the ladder rose.

'I want man-power! Come up and help me, Culley!'

140

No one could hear distinctly that far down, but Norman was already half way up the mast.

★

The chief engineer was not pleased to be woken: nor did he fully accept their explanation of an attempted suicide, but was convinced this was some drunken jape organized by the local land-owners after one of their notorious parties (to which he was not invited, not being 'accepted' by the district). He was however impressed by the fact that Tommy Mulligan—whom he knew to be a stalwart man although a drinker—had also fainted on reaching the foot of the mast, and that Mrs Bailey herself—who did not appear to him to be drunk—was still in a comatose condition. 'Well,' he said, 'I accept all you say, J G, but you'd better call this lady's husband and ask him to come and fetch her.'

'He isn't well either: I'll drive her back.'

'They're *both* not well when they give a big party? He must be drunk too,' said the chief, his suspicions once more rising.

'I keep telling you: nobody's drunk: it's just that this lady had a crisis and there was very nearly a most unfortunate accident.'

'Well, she can't stay here,' said the chief somewhat vindictively. 'We've no facilities for married quarters yet, as you know.'

'I said I'd drive her back. Just make sure, chief, you look after Tommy till I return.'

So filled with a sense of anti-climax and fatigue, J G set out again in his car for Cootamundra, with Maureen nursing Helen in the back, and Norman bringing up the rear in the heavy Armstrong-Siddeley. As they neared the junction where the road rose from Macnamara's, Norman was surprised to see a light coming up the hill and waited till the car caught up with him: it was once again Mrs Baxter in her runabout, its roof and rack now piled high with luggage.

He got out and spoke to her at the next gate as J G, intent on getting Mrs Bailey home, drove steadily, myopically on. 'Oh, it's you, Norman,' she said. 'What's to do?'

He related the drama of the evening, and Mrs Baxter, though herself distressed, found time to tut and shed a noiseless tear. 'The poor thing!' she said. 'Thank God you got to her before she committed that great error.'

'I didn't, it was Tommy.'

'But you seem to have helped: I dare say you're a good boy, Norman.'

'But what about you, Mrs Baxter? What the hell are you up to at this hour of night?'

'Me?' She let out a great nervous laugh. 'Me, boy? Me—I'm on my way to the capital.'

'What—now? Driving all through the night?'

'No . . . I'll stop at the township on the way—I've already phoned them through at the hotel. Then come morning-time, I'm off to the big city.'

'Why: you leaving Macnamara's?'

'And Macnamara, Norman: he's moved Nancy in.'

'Gawd—already? I didn't think he meant it.'

'He does and is . . . much good may it do him—and her. But me, Norm, I've got my pride: I'm not staying a night under *that* roof when she's in there.'

'So you pinched the car and left, then?' he said admiringly.

'No—he gave it to me: a farewell present for all my years of faithful service to him . . . or perhaps he wanted to get rid of me all the faster.'

'Well! Well—I don't know where *I'm* going to bed down to-night . . . When I've parked this bus, I suppose J G will drive me back to the radio once more in the small hours.'

Mrs Baxter reached out a hand and took Norman's bare arm. 'Why go back to the radio with J G, Norman?'

'What else do you suggest I do? Stay the night at Cootamundra?'

'No—stay the night at the township with yours sincerely.'

'With *you*, Mrs Baxter? Have a heart!'

'Not with *me*, Norman—in the same hotel as me but *with*

Miss Maureen, and next day I'll drive you both down with me to the capital.'

'Eh?'

'You and she—I'll drive you both far away from here.'

'But . . . well, will she want to?'

'Why not ask her?'

'Do you think so? But she won't want to leave Mrs Bailey . . .'

'If you ask me, she'll be glad to get away from Mrs Bailey for all time once she's safely delivered her back to Cootamundra . . .'

'But who will look after Helen?'

'What's wrong with her husband?'

'But he doesn't speak to her.'

'Well, he'll have to now, won't he?'

'I suppose so . . .' Norman pondered. 'And you think Maureen will come with me—now?'

'Try asking her.'

'But what will J G say?'

'To hell with J G. Boy! Are you losing heart? Don't you *want* that girl?'

Norman smacked his hand down on the door of Mrs Baxter's runabout. 'It *is* an idea, you know. And you'll . . . well, you'll encourage her to?'

'No . . . all *I* will do is be her chaperone.'

'What's that?'

'You'll see. Come on—get in that Armstrong-whatsername and let's get started.'

★

Yet again J G invaded the privacy of the annexe, this time banging firmly on the locked door. Walter arose, cross and rumpled, and gave no friendly welcome to J G. 'And what has happened *now*?' he cried. 'What further folly?'

'You wife's ill, Mr Bailey. I've got her here outside.'

'Ill?' Walter rubbed his eyes. 'There has been a long sickness, all these years . . .'

'No, no: Mr Bailey, prepare for a shock: Mrs Bailey tried to kill herself just now.'

'She too?' He peered out beyond J G. 'She's not hurt?'

'Shock, Mr Bailey. Do please come and help me get her into safety.'

Unshaven and bedraggled, Walter emerged into the half light of the dawn. He did not speak to Maureen, nor to the figures gathered at the edge of the circle of car lights, but helped J G Eaton carry his wife slowly into the annexe. He laid her on the horse-hair sofa, and looked into her eyes which opened. 'Ah, Helen,' he said. 'They tell me you've had an accident. Would you like some brandy?'

She nodded.

'Don't you think we need a doctor, Mr Bailey?'

'Do you need a doctor, Helen?'

She shook her head and took the glass.

'Then thank you, Eaton,' said Walter rising; and coming to the door added, 'And thank all you good people, whoever you may be.' Then he closed the door, leaving all four of them feeling rather like children who have interfered in adult undertakings.

'Ah well,' said J G, returning to briskness. 'We've done all that *we* can, without a doubt. You coming, Norman?'

'No—I'll come over in the morning.'

'Why? I must get back to make sure Tommy isn't damaged either . . .'

'I'll come in the morning: I could do with a bit of early breakfast, and I dare say Mrs Baxter could too before her journey.'

'Very well: I'll be off, then. All this goes to show'—J G paused beside his convertible—'that marriage is a serious matter: we should remember that. I shall tell Margaret what has happened and let's hope we can both learn from the misfortunes and mistakes of others.'

'Good on you, J G Eaton!' Mrs Baxter cried, slapping him on the back and almost shoving him into his car.

'Yes, well good-bye—and thank you all. You too, Maureen. I'll ring you tomorrow and see that all's well with you here.'

'Thanks, J G,' they all chorused, bustling him off . . . and he lurched and jerked down the drive and towards his distant destination.

'You two will want to talk a bit,' said Mrs Baxter. 'I'll sit waiting for you here, but don't be long: time presses, and I'm sleepy as I expect you are.'

Norman walked with Maureen up towards the house, and when they were out of sight of Mrs Baxter, he took her by the shoulders and said, 'You're coming with me, Maureen.'

'What, Norman?'

'Mrs Baxter's driving to the capital: she'll take us there with her.'

'What—now? And what about Mrs Bailey? I can't leave her here alone . . .'

'She's not alone: she's got her husband.'

'But you don't understand, Norman: they're not on speaking terms.'

'She's lying in his room: that's better than speaking terms.'

'But I can't just dash off without a word . . .'

'Listen, Maureen: the last person she'll want to see later this morning will be you.'

'And Nance has gone too! She'll have nobody.'

'Just as well she'll have nobody: she'll have her husband.'

'And what if they start fighting again?'

'Then she can find another girl, or girls—anyone but you.'

'Norman! You mean just walk out like that? Walk out of Cootamundra?'

'Ask yourself, Maureen: what *are* you doing here? And what *should* you be doing? You should be keeping your promise and coming to marry me!'

'When?'

'As soon as I've got your dad's permission—and your mum's.'

'Dad'll have a fit; and I don't know if my brothers will like you ...'

'Fuck your brothers: so long as you do—and perhaps your mum.'

'Come *now*, you say?'

'Yeah: *now*: what are we waiting for?'

She kissed him. 'I don't know,' she said. 'I'll go and pack a bag.'

'Just one ... you can have any other things sent on.'

'Okay: I'm coming.'

'You want some help?'

'No—wait for me down by Mrs Baxter's car.'

The house seemed already alien to Maureen, and she realized one of the first signs of growing up—or growing older—which is that places, which seemed so important—so much part of oneself and one's stability—can lose all their meaning when the meaning of one's life has altered suddenly.

Down by the car, Mrs Baxter yawned, lit a fag, and grew slightly cynical. 'You're really going to *marry* her, son, I hope,' she said.

'Of course. A wife, dad says, is much less expensive than a mistress—and the old man should know.'

'Try to treat your wife like one, all the same, son,' she declared. 'And whatever you do never try to humiliate a woman—that was Macnamara's big mistake, as he'll discover.'

'You think Nance will stick it out there?'

'As a matter of fact, I think she will. The question is going to be if *he* runs away from *her*.'

'You think old Nancy's got character, then?'

'She and he are much of a muchness, but don't forget she's younger. Ah, look! Here's your fiancée, soon to be the blushing bride.'

146

Maureen sat beside Mrs Baxter, and Norman wedged himself with her bag in the dickey seat.

'Farewell to Cootamundra!' cried Mrs Baxter gaily, 'and the district. And as for you, Norman, no back-seat driving, if you please. It's not *me* you're marrying, fortunately for you—and me —but this dark-eyed sheila here. Right! All set? We're off then, here we go!'

The sound of this last untoward departure brought Walter to the door again, where he stood against the light in pyjamas and bare feet. He gazed after the car, then across at his silent dark ancestral home. Picking up a book and a torch, he walked gingerly across the buffalo-grass, sniffing the air with his face upturned to a sky where the bright stars were no longer visible, except in clustered patches. Reaching the rain-gauge, he lifted the filter and examined the measured glass: there were a few faint drops of water in its base.

He sniffed these two, then replaced the filter, made an entry in his book, and returned across the grass to the annexe. Helen, he found, was sitting up on the sofa arranging her hair. 'Thank you, Walter,' she said quietly. 'As I expect you've heard, I did try to behave rather foolishly.'

'Yes,' he said. 'So I did hear. Don't you want to sleep now?'

'Not yet, Walter. I want to explain to somebody.'

'That is, to me?'

'Yes, Walter: that is, if you're prepared to listen.'

Walter put down his book, poured two more brandies, and said, 'I think we might forego all explanations, Helen. Life is its own explanation: the rest is just words, usually.'

'All the same, Walter . . . you heard I tried to kill myself?'

'Yes: I did.'

'Does the reason why interest you?'

'I know it: you were in love with a boy . . . I watched you both together by the dam . . .'

'Oh, you saw us there? Why didn't you . . . ?'

'Intervene?'

'Yes . . .'

'I "intervened", as a matter of fact, by trying to blow my brains out, and failing to.'

'No, Walter!'

'Yes, Helen. Please observe that portrait of my grandfather.'

Her eyes strayed but did not look. 'Because you were . . . well, anxious about me?'

'No, not exactly: because I was in despair about myself.'

'Because of me?'

'Because of myself: my life: all its failures . . .'

'But seeing *me* drove you to this?'

'It did . . . And seeing what, Helen, drove *you* to *your* particular folly?'

'This boy and Maureen made love . . . I wasn't spying, I just happened to see it. It seems one doesn't need to spy, Walter. What fate wants you to see to cause you pain, it will always arrange for you to do so . . .'

'So it would seem . . .'

'Yes . . .'

They looked at each other, the guards dropping, but the incomprehension just as total. 'We seem to have come to a dead end, Walter,' she said.

'Well—nearly a dead end. I think you should try to sleep now.'

'Very well: I'll go back to the house . . .'

'You can stay here if you wish: I shall be getting up . . .'

'Here? I've never stayed here since you moved in, Walter . . . And how long ago was that?'

'Too long ago . . . it doesn't matter . . . it's too late to . . .'

'Why, Walter, must it always be too late?'

'Perhaps we both want it to be so.'

'Oh no, I don't believe we do . . . Oh no, I don't believe we always did . . . Something came between us and our dearest wishes, Walter . . . something cruel and terrible and remorseless . . . Tell me—what was it?'

He stood up. 'Helen, this conversation will lead nowhere, but I believe this "it" was you.'

'I caused my misery?'

'And mine.'

'You don't think I've suffered?'

'I do think you have, and I do think that you've wanted to: perhaps unconsciously, but wanted to.'

'How?'

'Oh, Helen! Why dig up a past we were managing to bury? How? By refusing to be my wife—that was all—that was how . . .'

'But I've not deserted you, Walter.'

'Because you needed me: needed my absent presence; but that is not being a *wife* . . .'

'What is? Love? But I *have* loved you, Walter; I still do wish to love you now!'

'*Oh yes* . . .'

'Yes, I did and do. I gave myself to you—can you deny this, Walter?'

'Helen: what you call "give yourself" is merely an inflated term for doing what any honest wife, who freely takes a man, would agree to do . . . would be glad to do. But alas, the way you "gave" yourself showed to me all too clearly that my body disgusted you.'

'No, Walter! No, no, it was *not* that—there-you-are-mistaken! It was not your body I rejected, nor your love. It was just that the love *I* was possessed of—the love I wanted to give wholly, entirely, utterly and forever—found no echo in your heart—it was too great for you!'

'Oh Helen, these are just words! I am I—Walter Bailey of Cootamundra station. What I am and have I offered to you fully —myself and all I am and have and love. More than that I could not; and if you say I did not, you were asking of me—perhaps asking of any man, asking of life itself—more than ever can be given.'

'Yes . . .'

'And so?'

'Yes . . . Perhaps I should have had patience, Walter, and subdued my yearning for an absolute till time taught me I could find it there beside me . . .'

'Ah, Helen! If you'd said or thought or acted on that twenty, ten, even five years ago!'

'And now it's too late?'

'It's too late, yes, because we are both too old for passion, too wounded by the years . . .'

'To old in our bodies?'

'I don't think so . . . too old in our hearts . . .'

'Is it even now too late?' she said, starting to hold out her arms.

He looked at her, and smiled sourly. 'Helen,' he said, 'don't speak to me like a harlot: be true, at any rate, to the great error you have committed—of asking too much, by your arrogance and unreality, from this world . . .'

Tears flowed from her eyes, but not those of hysteria. 'I suppose you would say I have wronged you, Walter,' she said, looking at him.

'Yes . . .'

'And you will never see, then, that *I* have been wronged by life which told me love should be so wonderful, and wrought from me the promise I would make *any* sacrifice if I could find a love that matched my own?'

'Yes: I see that: with your great unreasoning heart, Helen, you too must feel you have been wronged . . .'

He approached and stroked her hair distractedly (and with slightly trembling fingers) as she gazed up at him with that look of innocence that had always confounded him because of its betrayal (to her and so to him) of all reality . . .

150

'I must dress now,' he said. 'A mundane matter, but I'm going to see to the cows ... So life continues: cows, water, grass —the dull and endless processes of nature. Perhaps, at our ages we should learn from that eternal stupidity, and not torture each other with impossibilities. I have failed you, Helen, because I am myself. You have failed yourself and me for the same reason. Let us accept your loss is the greater; and your personality, though I think it's disastrously dishonest, to be at any rate one unique, entire, and therefore admirable ... Let us not try to hurt each other any longer, nor regret, nor hope in vain ...'

She looked at him with those wide still so lovely eyes that had always captivated him and said, 'I do feel for you, Walter, and no one would ever have behaved to me so well as you. But I shall never cease to hope so long as I live ...'

'Hope,' Walter said, 'is the great source of life, and the great and terrible deceiver ...'

He left her: and when he came back half an hour later, showered and dressed, he found her sleeping. He touched her gently, with dry tears in his eyes, then lifted her easily and carried her out into the late night. The silhouettes of the trees were now visible, and a light rain fell as he walked with her slowly over to the house. There he carried her up to her bedroom, laid her gently on the huge empty bed, and dried her hair and body with the counterpane. He opened the window slightly, and took the two photographs of their young selves; lifted them up and gazed at them, looked back at her, then put them softly down in the same places where he had found them.

THE HOGARTH PRESS

A New Life For A Great Name

This is a paperback list for today's readers – but it holds to a tradition of adventurous and original publishing set by Leonard and Virginia Woolf when they founded The Hogarth Press in 1917 and started their first paperback series in 1924.

Now, after many years of partnership, Chatto & Windus · The Hogarth Press are proud to launch this new series. Our choice of books does not echo that of the Woolfs in every way – times have changed – but our aims are the same. Some sections of the list are light-hearted, some serious: all are rigorously chosen, excellently produced and energetically published, in the best Hogarth Press tradition. We hope that the new Hogarth Press paperback list will be as prized – and as avidly collected – as its illustrious forebear.

A list of our books already published, together with some of our forthcoming titles, follows. If you would like more information about Hogarth Press books, write to us for a catalogue:

40 William IV Street, London WC2N 4DF

Please send a large stamped addressed envelope

HOGARTH FICTION

Behind A Mask: The Unknown Thrillers of Louisa May Alcott
Edited and Introduced by Madeleine Stern

Death of a Hero by Richard Aldington
New Introduction by Christopher Ridgway

The Amazing Test Match Crime by Adrian Alington
New Introduction by Brian Johnston

Epitaph of a Small Winner by Machado de Assis
Translated and Introduced by William L. Grossman

Mrs Ames by E.F. Benson
Paying Guests by E.F. Benson
Secret Lives by E.F. Benson
New Introductions by Stephen Pile

Ballantyne's Folly by Claud Cockburn
New Introduction by Andrew Cockburn
Beat the Devil by Claud Cockburn
New Introduction by Alexander Cockburn

Chance by Joseph Conrad
New Introduction by Jane Miller

Lady Into Fox & *A Man in the Zoo* by David Garnett
New Introduction by Neil Jordan

The Whirlpool by George Gissing
New Introduction by Gillian Tindall

Morte D'Urban by J.F. Powers
Prince of Darkness and other stories by J.F. Powers
New Introductions by Mary Gordon

Mr Weston's Good Wine by T.F. Powys
New Introduction by Ronald Blythe

The Revolution in Tanner's Lane by Mark Rutherford
New Introduction by Claire Tomalin
Catharine Furze by Mark Rutherford
Clara Hopgood by Mark Rutherford
New Afterwords by Claire Tomalin

The Last Man by Mary Shelley
New Introduction by Brian Aldiss

The Island of Desire by Edith Templeton
Summer in the Country by Edith Templeton
New Introductions by Anita Brookner

Christina Alberta's Father by H.G. Wells
Mr Britling Sees It Through by H.G. Wells
New Introductions by Christopher Priest

Frank Burnet by Dorothy Vernon White
New Afterword by Irvin Stock